BUILT BY MAGIC

BUILT BY MAGIC

JENNA WOLFHART

For the orc lovers

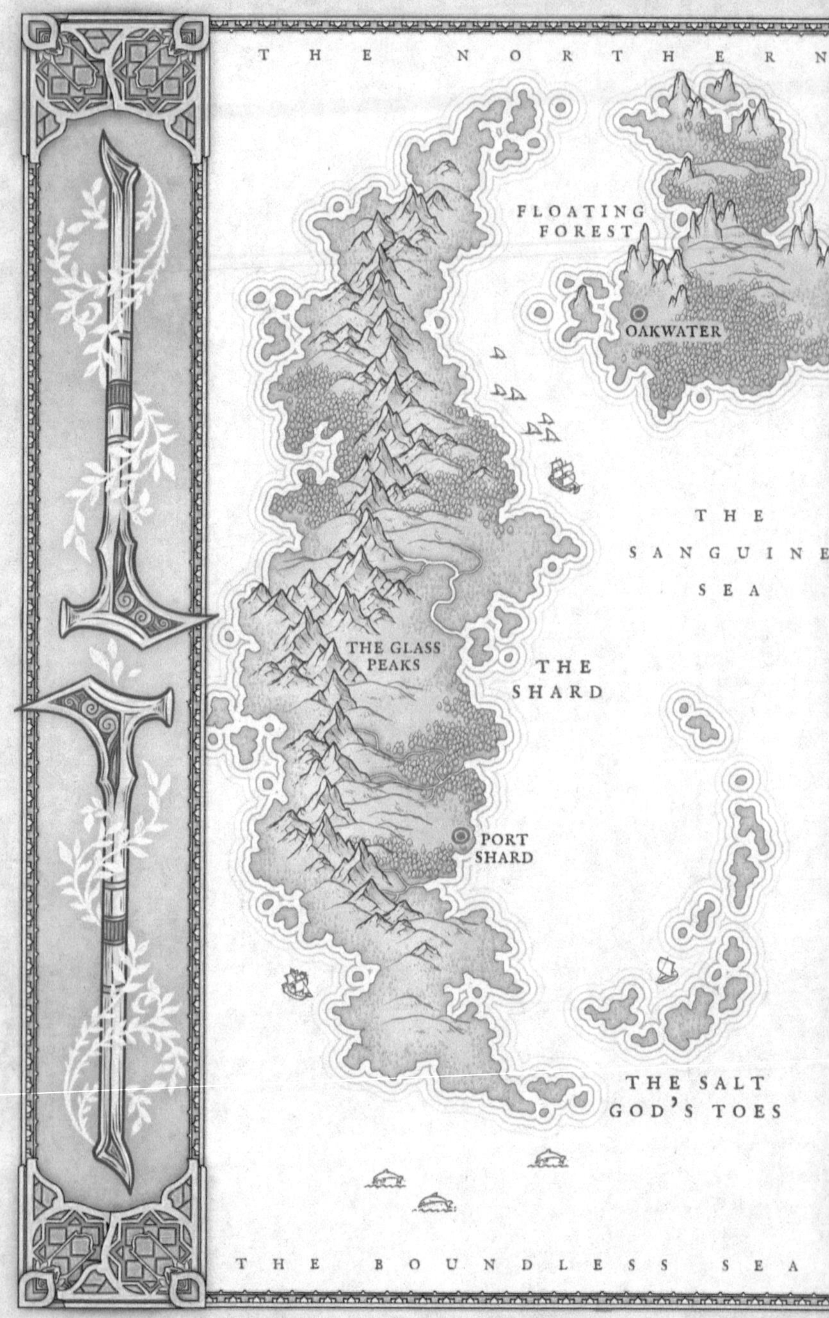

THE NORTHERN
FLOATING FOREST
OAKWATER
THE SANGUINE SEA
THE GLASS PEAKS
THE SHARD
PORT SHARD
THE SALT GOD'S TOES
THE BOUNDLESS SEA

OCEAN
THE ISLES OF
FABLE
CASTLE RUINS
SUNLIT RIDGE
RIVERWOLD
MILFORD
WHISPERING WOODS
ASHBORN FOREST
MOUNT FORGE
WYNDALE
HEARTHAVEN

I

FRIDA

I balanced on the sloped rooftop, aiming the tip of my arrow at my prey. My heartbeat was a steady beat beneath my ribs that counted down the seconds I had left to take my shot. A gentle breeze pushed into the courtyard, dashing my mark's yellow hair into his flat eyes, momentarily blinding him. I smiled. My opportunity would get no better than this.

I steadied my aim, squinting beneath the orange glare of the evening sun, and the bowstring went taut. Breathing calm and mind clear, I checked the sight one last time, then loosed. The arrow hissed through the air, spinning away from me. Only two heartbeats later, the sharp tip punched into my target's soft, squishy head. A spray of black sand exploded from his face.

I leapt to my feet and threw my fisted hand into the air, a celebratory shout bursting from my lungs. Down in the courtyard-turned-arena below, several leather-clad figures wandered out from the protected observation stand, washed in the sunset's glow. A few lifted their bows and aimed up at me.

Smiling, I slid down the sloped rust-red tiles in the opposite direction, and launched onto the ground, where I landed in a crouch. City dust plumed around me. My horse, a mare named Stella, neighed and shook her long black mane around her powerful shoulders. I leapt onto her back and urged her through the streets.

As her hooves thundered across the cobbles, wind tore through my hair and an exhilarating sense of *rightness* settled over me. Heart pounding, I leaned forward, my hands against her slick neck, using my decade-long practice to keep my balance. A sense of wild freedom filled my chest, the drab city nothing but a whorl of nothingness surrounding me. I was loath to turn her back toward the courtyard, but I had no other choice. The others were waiting for me.

Because somehow, I'd done it.

I'd actually passed. That meant I was now an official member of the guild. Which was *amazing.* Dreams do come true.

But an unexpected tremor of unease went

through me as I turned Stella back around. It was all quite sudden, really. I'd expected it to take more than a year for me to earn a coveted spot in the most infamous guild on the continent. That would have meant at least a few more months of freedom before I was bound to them for the rest of my very long life. As an elf, that meant centuries. Apparently, it had taken my brother a full three years before he'd passed his induction. For some recruits, it took even longer.

But, of course, I'd been an archer all my life, which had given me an edge. My mother had handed me a miniature bow before I'd even taken my first step.

Besides, this was what I *wanted*. My mother had served in the guild before her illness. My father still did, along with my brother, my uncle, and my cousins. The Assassin's Guild was a family affair, and I wouldn't be the first Rurik to turn her back on it forever.

When I returned to the courtyard and dismounted, several figures were waiting for me. All politely clapped, save my brother, Logi, who whooped and hollered. A little over a year ago, he'd come to me and had begged me to join the guild. And when I'd finally relented, he'd spent every spare moment of his time training me.

"Yes, Fri!" he shouted, his long chestnut hair a wild tangle around his broad shoulders.

Behind him, I spotted my father striding through the makeshift obstacles with a twinkle in his eye. The black leathers he wore signified his spot as a high-ranking member of the guild and gave his muscular form a dangerous edge.

"I don't think any of us doubted you could do it, but well done, Frida. Excellent archery skills, as always," he said in that great booming way of his. His voice always struck me as the complete antithesis of everything else he was. When he wore his assassin role, he rarely spoke. And if he did, his words were whispered, barely loud enough for one to hear. His skills of stealth were something of a legend around these parts. He liked to say the assassin was a mask he wore to hide the loud, thundering mass of a man he truly was.

Although I sometimes wondered if it wasn't the other way around—if the assassin was the real him, deep down. To me, it didn't matter either way. I loved both sides of him.

"Thanks, Father," I said, beaming at his praise.

"Yes, well done, well done," came the nasally voice of the elf who was the true leader of the guild. Erik was the head of the Conung family, who also led the Thieves' Guild. It made him the most powerful person in the elven kingdom, after the queen. Although many considered his power to exceed even hers.

It did in the streets, at least.

He wore his long silver hair slicked back and tied into an agonizingly tight bun that made it look like his skin was being yanked off his face. His head-to-toe garments were a mottled gray—the color signifying him as our leader. He said it was the best color for blending in with the city's cobbled streets and drab buildings. Wearing his trademark sneer, he looked up and down the length of me, like I was some kind of undesirable who'd wandered in from beyond the guild's gated walls. Someone who didn't belong.

"I suppose I should congratulate you," he said after a moment. "But you do understand you're not a full member of the guild just yet?"

My father frowned. "Of course she is. Her arrow hit the target, and she got away before any of our own archers could retaliate. She successfully completed her induction task."

"She shot a scarecrow in an entirely fake scenario. It's hardly a true test of her ability to stay calm under pressure. We need to see her in action —*real* action. None of this darting around rooftops and shooting inanimate objects."

Hands fisting, I lifted my chin. "I don't understand. You're the one who set this task for me."

"Yes, and your passing means you can now be considered a guild member on *a trial basis*," he said firmly, in a voice that brooked no argument. "Now you may be given your first quest. Complete it successfully, and you'll officially be one of us."

I looked to my father. His brow was furrowed, but he slowly nodded, clearly agreeing with Erik, which frustrated me to no end. I'd done everything he'd asked of me. I'd completed all my training and had devoted the past year of my life to them, even following their ways of celibacy and sobriety, despite my reluctance. And I'd now succeeded at the induction task, the same one every other member had once been given. No one had been required to do an additional trial quest. Until now.

"Hmm," my father said, scratching his chin. "I suppose it's a fair requirement."

My jaw nearly dropped. "Wait, you agree with him? But why?"

When I'd first shown up on the guild's doorstep, my father had been delighted. More than anything, he wanted me to join. Or at least I thought he had.

"It's only right we test new members—out in the field, where it matters. In fact, I think we should make this a permanent rule going forward. For all new recruits." He smiled serenely at Erik. "Wouldn't you agree?"

Ah. I saw what he was doing. He'd agree to hoisting a new, unexpected rule on me, but only if Erik confirmed that everyone else must go through the same paces. And I supposed it wasn't so bad. Sooner or later—likely on the sooner side, knowing how fast things moved around here—I'd have been sent off on my first quest, anyway. I just had to make sure I nailed this one, so Erik would have no excuse to turn me away at the end of it.

Erik flattened his lips into a thin line, then said, "Yes, of course. From now on, we'll give all new members a trial quest to see how they perform in a real world scenario."

My father nodded. "Good. Frida, do you wish to proceed?"

"I suppose," I said. "What do you need me to do?"

Erik smiled, turned, and motioned at one of the many guards he kept stationed around the guild's grounds. The guard, donned in deep red leathers, lifted a folded piece of parchment and hastened across the courtyard. As I waited to hear the details of my mission, my stomach twisted uncomfortably, like angry sea waves had taken up residence inside me. I fought the urge to swipe my sweaty palms against my trousers. Erik, I had to admit, might have a bit of a point with the whole trial period thing.

Because the idea of actually aiming my arrow at someone and watching the life bleed from their eyes...well, I just thought I'd have more time before I had to do it, that was all. Time to steel myself against it. I'd never felt eager to kill. It was why I'd held off joining for so long. But my brother had convinced me that I'd feel differently once I got involved. We didn't kill anyone who was worth saving, after all. Only the bastards of the world, who deserved what they got.

Really, the guild was doing a good thing for society, and no matter what happened, I would only aim the tip of my arrow at someone who deserved it.

But knowing that didn't mean I felt ready. Maybe I just needed to get the first one over with. Maybe then it wouldn't feel like my insides were being shoved through a cheese grater.

The guard came to a stop beside Erik. Reverently, he held the paper in his upraised palms and held it toward me. Swallowing, I took the offered task, unfolded the parchment, and gobbled the words with my eyes.

Assassin's Guild Assignment for Frida Rurik

An orc named Rune—surname unknown—is rumored to live on the Floating Forest, a small island located within the Isles of Fable. There, he keeps a dragon. To complete your induction, track down this orc and take his dragon. Assassination is not required.

Heart pounding, I read the impossible words again.

To complete your induction, track down this orc and take his dragon.

I blinked, then looked up. "Is this a joke?"

"Why would it be a joke?" Erik asked, practically purring.

My blood began to boil. He'd done this on purpose. He'd given me an insurmountable task, knowing I'd never succeed—which meant I'd be locked out of the guild for the rest of my life. I shook my head in disbelief. What had I ever done to him? It felt like he'd been against me from the start.

"All the dragons are dead," I said flatly.

He smiled, though there was no warmth in the expression. "That's not true. I know you've heard the rumors about the four dragons living on those islands."

"There's also a rumor that Isveig's ghost is trapped in chains, wandering the world in pain for all of eternity. But everyone knows that's nothing more than a fanciful tale. Same as this." I waved the parchment in the air to punctuate my statement.

Isveig had been a conqueror who had hunted and killed both orcs and dragons alike, all in his quest for power. Thankfully, the orcs had retaken their kingdom nearly thirty years ago. He'd rotted in the dungeons for a long while. But he was dead now. Good riddance.

I often wished the tales were true and his soul was cursed to endure a miserable half-existence for eternity, but ghosts didn't exist. And neither did dragons—unfortunately.

"I have it on good authority that these dragons are very much alive," Erik said, then shrugged. "But if you aren't up for the task, I'll find someone else to do it."

Fuck. He was serious about this, and judging by his expression, he actually believed in these dragons. If I didn't agree to this, he'd force me to pack my bag, walk out those gates, and never look back. I might not even get a chance to say my goodbyes —not properly. He'd given me no choice but to accept this doomed mission. And when I inevitably failed...well, I'd worry about that when the time came.

My father's frown had deepened over the course of the conversation until his expression had transformed into an outright scowl. "When you brought up this new trial period, I thought you'd have her go for a target in the city. Or at least on the continent. This assignment will take weeks—if not more. And you don't even want her to assassinate the target?"

Erik sniffed and looked down his nose at my father. "We've been hired to do a job, and that job is to take the dragon from him. That is why she's going to the Isles."

"I thought they were pro—"

"You thought right. No harm will be done," Eric said, a tense gaze locked on my father's face. "This is the assignment I've decided to give Frida. Go to the island, harm no one, and bring me that dragon." He slid his gaze toward me. "Take it or leave it."

For one heart-pounding moment, I actually considered saying no. I could walk away from all this and go back to my cottage in the woods that I'd held on to this past year, just in case things fell apart at the guild and I needed to return home. But the truth was, I was lonely out there by myself. I had Stella, of course, but all of my loved ones were here.

Guild members were forbidden from fraternizing with those outside the organization. Before I'd come to the city with my tail between my legs, I'd gone years without seeing my brother and my father. Birthday gifts had mysteriously turned up on my front porch, but that had been the extent of their contact. And since my nearest neighbors lived miles away, it'd been just me for a really long time.

It felt good to be a part of something again—to feel like I had a real family now—even if I wasn't completely thrilled about how I had to earn my place with them.

And so I couldn't say no. Not when it meant going back to that aching loneliness again. At least I didn't have to assassinate anyone yet.

"Frida?" Erik asked, his silver brow arching.

I wound my hands around my back and fidgeted with my tunic's bottom hemline. The material was rough and scratchy, but it was something to hold on to.

"No, I'll do it. I accept the mission," I said, my voice tight. "I just have one question, if that's all right."

"Very well," he said.

"Someone has hired us to steal a dragon. What do they want with it?"

Erik levelled his dark gaze on me. "I can imagine many reasons why one would want a dragon, but it is not our business to ask questions of those who hire our services."

I prickled at that. "That's not true. We ask questions all the time—to make sure we're aiming our sights on the right people. Just because we're assassins for hire doesn't mean we're willing to spill the blood of an innocent. Not anymore. We turned aside from the ways of the old guild decades ago."

"This was a mistake," Erik snapped, turning to my father. "I told you she wasn't ready."

"And *I* told you she was," my father replied in a voice that held just as much snap. Then he turned to me. "I'm sure we were hired to get the dragon away from someone dangerous. You'll be doing the world a favor by taking it from the mark. Any more than that, we can't tell you. And if this goes wrong, I'm afraid you won't get another chance to join the guild."

Unspoken demand: *stop asking questions*. It was a blunt command, one I knew he would never take back.

I searched his eyes for any indication of what he was thinking. Something about this entire situation felt off to me, but if my father agreed with Erik, I supposed I'd have to do it. He'd never send me on an assignment he thought I'd fail, and he'd certainly never let something as powerful as a dragon end up in the wrong hands. I truly believed that.

And so when he gave me a slow nod, I forced myself to stand tall.

"All right," I said. "When do I leave?"

Erik's slow smile chilled me to my bones. "In one hour. Gather your things. The ship will be waiting for you in the harbor."

2

FRIDA

I looked around my room one last time, wondering if I'd ever see it again. The barren, stone-walled enclosure was a striking contrast to my cottage hidden away in the lush forest, with its large, flung-wide windows and worn timber floors that creaked under every step, like the house itself was alive and speaking back to me. Letting me know it was there to hold me in its warm, cozy embrace.

The lodgings of the Assassin's Guild were cold and windowless, situated inside a skinny hall that had once been a prison for undesirables. I'd been forced to leave most of my belongings back home, bringing only the bare necessities with me when I moved here to train. The guild didn't believe in frivolities—things like perfumed soaps, handmade pottery overflowing with lush plants, and stacks of fiction books that smelled of ink and vellum. Everything I truly loved was still there—everything but my family—and I'd left it the way I liked it, just in case I failed here.

But deep down, I knew failure wasn't an option.

With a sigh, I threw a worn leather pack onto my shoulder, along with my bow and arrows, and left the barren room and its insufferably thin straw mattress behind. Once I was back outside with the fresh air filling my lungs and the cerulean sky stretching overhead, my heartbeat cantered at the thought of the adventure looming before me. After a full year, I could finally have some time away from this dreary city and those lifeless guild-hall rooms. I hated leaving my family and Stella, but I couldn't think of a single other thing I'd miss about this place. Except maybe the owlery, where I'd spent a large portion of my time tending to the birds when they returned from delivering messages.

I took off toward the docks with a pep in my step. But as I made my way through the bustling city streets, it felt like a noose was wrapped around my throat—one controlled by Erik. Because though I might spend the next month or two out in the wilds, the guild would draw me back to it eventually.

Which was fine—no, *good*. It was what I wanted, wasn't it?

This was the life I'd chosen. I had to see this thing through.

Weeks passed in a haze of sunshine and salt-thick air. I spent my days wandering the deck and helping the crew with whatever tasks they needed. At times, I stood on the bow and gazed ahead into the endless stretch of blue, my heart a wild thing in my chest. My emotions were more at odds than they'd ever been before. The blood in my veins seemed to hum from the thrill of the adventure, but my dread grew with every inch that vanished between me and our destination. Because once I arrived on the island, gone would be the soul-settling days of hard physical work and nights of booming laughter around bowls of salted fish and rice. In its place would come...well, at least it wasn't *murder*.

Yet.

The assignment parchment burned a hole in my pocket. I'd read it over and over again during the journey. It said not to kill the mark, but I couldn't help but wonder if that was part of the test. Would Erik welcome me into the guild if I showed up without my first assassination notched into my leather belt? Knowing him, it was hard to believe he'd accept anything but a full demonstration of my allegiance to the guild, above all else.

But if that was what he wanted, he should have said. As it was, I'd do what he asked and no more.

I tried not to dwell on it and focused on each day as it came, and eventually, the ship set its anchor down in the calm waters off the southwest coast of an island called the Floating Forest. From what I could tell at this distance, it was about as blunt as a name could be. Towering redwood trees with enormous trunks and rich, verdant leaves consumed the entire coast, backlit by a golden sun. A small stretch of beach hovered near the edge of the trees, where the waves gently lapped against pristine white sand.

The captain of the ship, an ice giant named Louisa, swaggered across the deck to where I stood gazing out at the island. At a staggering eight feet, she towered over me. Her long silver hair was braided down her back, and the sunlight illuminated her pale blue skin. An enormous hawk perched on her shoulder, ruffling his feathers. I rarely saw her without him.

"We're ready to lower the boat down for you," she said in the lilting accent of the northern mountains. "Head for that beach. You'll find a trail through the woods that will take you into Oakwater."

I nodded. The ship would go no closer to Oakwater, for fear of being spotted. If the islanders discovered this ship was in league with the guild, they'd likely cease all trade with them. I'd need to come and go as stealthily as possible.

Truth was, I'd come to know Louisa well over the past sixteen days, and she didn't strike me as the type to get involved with someone like Erik. She was all smiles most of the time and ensured her crew had plenty of hearty food and enough time for rest after long days spent toiling in the sun. Every night, she shared the table with us, laughing and joking and telling tales of her time spent on the sea. She also refused to do business with anyone who had a 'black heart' as she called it.

"Thanks for all your help. I've had a lovely time with you and your crew," I told her.

She cocked her head. "This is your first assignment, isn't it?"

I gave her a wry smile. "Is it that obvious?"

"I've only dealt with a few of you over the years. It's the kind of job I only take when trades are extremely slow," she said. "The others were nothing like you. They kept to themselves most of the time, and they had a certain *look* about them. Like they were immune to the charms of the sea.

But you're full of life. And they weren't." She patted me on the arm. "Whatever you've come here to do, try not to let it kill you, too, eh?"

My heart pounded against my ribs. If Erik found out she'd said this to me, he'd be livid. My friendliness had made her comfortable around me—too comfortable. And suddenly, I understood the guild's rules a little more than I had before. Connections were dangerous. For everyone involved.

I'd been born to become an assassin. It was in my blood. Running away from that life before had caused me nothing but pain. And if I had to shut down a part of my nature to get through these assignments, that was what I'd have to do, I supposed. It was the only way to keep my family in my life.

"I'll be fine," I told her after a long moment of silence stretched between us, interrupted only by the rush of waves against the ship.

She gave me a sad smile. "All right. Well, all I can do is wish you luck."

By the time I made it to shore, the deep blue haze of twilight had descended upon the island. The dark waters hissed against the sand as

I tugged the rowboat into the dense brush. I'd leave it hidden away, where I hoped no one would find it. Louisa would return with her ship in three weeks after she'd traded with the nearest island, The Shard. If I wasn't ready to leave, she'd sail off again, only to return two weeks after that. In the meantime, I'd have to wait it out in the wilds.

Not a problem. I'd spent so many years living in my rustic cottage, surrounded by trees and wild animals, that the forest felt more like home to me than anywhere else.

After I drowned my boat in a pile of leaves, I found the trail cutting through the redwoods and started off toward Oakwater. According to the guild's information, Rune lived on the outskirts of the village rather than in the town itself, a fact that would make my task a lot easier. The fewer possible witnesses, the better.

As my boots thudded against the packed dirt trail, twilight deepened into full night. Insects filled the forest with a buzzing melody, and the rustle of leaves and branches seemed to dog my every step. Out of the corner of my eye, I spotted a squirrel scrabble up the side of a tree, its eyes gleaming even in the heavy darkness. My elven senses seemed to heighten more at night, and the rich woody scents of the forest flooded over me. Moss and pine cones. Lichen and damp soil. Wild mint and petrichor.

A twang went through my stomach. Fate be damned, it smelled so much like *home*.

Soon, wood smoke curled through the trees, and the path widened, where it led toward several timber buildings. Their windows held a yellowish glow that battled with the forest shadows. I slowed and stepped off the path to melt into the trees. With a light footfall, I crept closer to the buildings.

Beyond the windows, a family of dwarves was gathered around a rustic wooden table and eating a hearty meal of stew. The two fathers sat on either end with their six children filling the chairs between them. The oldest boy, a lad of nine or ten, looked like he was regaling his family with a raucous tale while he played his lute furiously. His family listened with rapt attention, and after a time, everyone broke out into applause.

I crept closer, as if an invisible string was tugging me toward them. *This* was what a family truly was, the kind I'd never had. What if I'd never run away from mine all those years ago, before they'd moved into the guild-hall, where everything felt stark and cold? Could it have been like this if I'd stayed?

Could we have all gathered around the dinner table, sharing stories and songs?

No. My gut clenched. My parents had hidden the truth about the guild from me. So had my brother. Dinners had always been tense and burdened by endless secrets, me on the outside while the rest of them exchanged weighted, knowing looks. For a long time, I'd thought it was because none of them liked me very much, and they couldn't wait for me to go to bed so they could have a nice evening without me.

So one day, I'd crept from my room after my mother had put me to bed. I'd been so determined to catch them in the act—laughing together about annoying little Frida.

I hadn't overheard them talking about me, though. That was the night I'd discovered every single member of my family, past and present, was a killer.

It was the night I'd packed my bags and fled the city. I'd run for hours that night until I'd stumbled upon an abandoned cottage in the woods, the floorboards coated in a thick layer of dust.

The memories from that night made my heart ache, even after all this time.

Sighing, I put my back to the dwarven family and walked shakily through the trees. My arms ached from the row across the sea, and I couldn't remember the last time I'd eaten. As eager as I was to find Rune, I needed rest. I should find somewhere to make camp, get some sleep, and search for his home in the early morning hours before the sun rose.

I backtracked, heading away from the tree line. I wouldn't risk staying in close proximity to civilization tonight, nor would I risk a fire. After a while, I came across a tree hollow, the hole large enough for me to fit comfortably. Seemed like as good a spot as any.

After I settled inside the trunk with my back against the rough wood, I dug through my pack. My provisions were enough for tonight, but I'd need to forage and hunt tomorrow, especially if I wanted to keep my energy up. A few bits of dried meat would soothe the hungry ache in my stomach for now, but it wouldn't go much further than that.

When I was done eating, I shrugged off my cloak, folded it into a pillow, and curled up against the inside of the tree. I thought it would take a while for me to settle enough for sleep, but I hadn't accounted for how heavily my exhaustion weighed on me. And within moments, the world of dreams greeted me.

Gone were my dark thoughts of barren rooms, gray walls, and dagger-wielding killers. Instead, I dreamed of sunshine and laughter. Of bare feet on mossy earth and the rich scent of redwoods.

3

RUNE

My wards pinged, jingling the silver bell hanging above my door. Frowning, I lifted my eyes from the open book on my lap—I'd been engrossed in a murder mystery, where twelve strangers were trapped in a storm-swept castle together—and glared out the window. What in fate's name had tripped them now? This was happening an obnoxious amount lately, and I couldn't figure out how to fix it. Forest critters weren't supposed to set off my wards, and yet there they went again.

Grumbling, I snapped my book shut and placed it on the table next to my rocking chair. The fire raged in the hearth, blasting a soothing heat through my cottage. The spring weather had warmed the past few weeks, but I liked it hot.

"I better go fucking check on it, Moira," I muttered to the black cat perched on my kitchen table, licking her paw. She stared at me with glittering eyes, like she was daring me to tell her to get off the table again. I'd given up. The damn beast owned this cottage at this point.

I thundered over to the door, unlatched it, and yanked it open. "You coming?"

She very pointedly continued to stare. Unlike every other cat I'd met—which to be fair, wasn't all that many—Moira hated going out at night. If I tried to encourage her, she hissed at me and all her hair stood on end, like I was asking her to stand out in the rain or something.

"Ridiculous cat," I muttered, then ventured outside.

It was a warm spring night, insects buzzing, moths bouncing against the window. I moved toward the woods. A few rabbits darted away at my heavy footsteps, and I could feel one of the neighborhood owls watching me. I fed them sometimes, and they were getting bolder by the day, which was all well and good so long as Moira didn't come out once the sun went down. She'd try to catch one, though I couldn't say she'd be particularly successful. She was a funny little thing. All hiss and no bite.

The redwoods towered around my cottage, boxing it in so that my home almost seemed like it was a part of the forest, which was what I liked most about it. Most inhabitants of this island lived in the town of Oakwater, about a half hour's walk from here. They insisted on clustering together like that, nearly living on top of each other. Windows looked into neighboring windows, and voices drifted through walls, enough for you to make out every word of someone's conversation. They were packed in tight, even when there was all this *space*. I didn't see much sense in living like that.

No matter. It meant no one came looking to build their house anywhere near mine.

My ward suddenly pinged again, and the bell's jingle drifted toward me through the open door.

Frowning, I hefted my axe from the ground and ventured into the thick of the forest. It probably didn't mean anything. It never did. But I couldn't ignore it, either. Because the first time I brushed it aside would be the time it really mattered.

With the axe head resting on my shoulder, I strode through the familiar trees, not even looking as I cut my path toward the perimeter I'd marked with my Jordur sand. The sand was one of the four Galdur elements, one of the few true aspects of magic in the world. Most folk didn't know the full depths of what the sand could do, but I'd spent my youth at an academy for those interested in training magic. And the Jordur sand, the element of the earth, could be worked in such a way that it could warn its user of intruders, so long as said intruder crossed the line of sand.

When I'd buried it in a circular formation around my cottage, I'd known windswept leaves and forest critters could be a problem, so I'd followed the instructions in a textbook I'd...'borrowed' from the academy. It was meant to alert me only when the intruder was over a certain size.

It had always worked until recently. Seven times now, it had pinged when nothing was there.

Odds were, nothing was there this time, either. But I still had to check. It was the only warning I'd get if someone found me. And even though none of them should be able to step foot on this island, I knew they'd find a workaround one day.

I stalked through the trees, my axe at the ready. The scent of wood smoke permeated the forest, drowning out the usual scents of pine, moss, and fragrant wildflowers, thicker now that I was away from my cottage. I frowned and looked in the direction of my closest neighbors. A family of dwarves had taken up residence about a ten-minute walk from here, but they didn't usually burn logs this time of year. They were more comfortable when there was a chill in the air, having lived most of their lives underground in the caves of The Glass Peaks.

Unease rattled through me. The dwarves were good folk. When they'd first arrived on the island, they hadn't turned their noses up at living near me, despite me being a full-blooded orc. And when they'd asked me to build their home for them, I'd been more than happy to oblige. I might not be a talkative sort with a lot of friends, but I did what I could for those who needed me.

If that fire was coming from their place...there could have been an accident.

I took off, sprinting through the trees with my axe hanging heavily by my side. Within moments, I'd erased the distance between our homes. I peered through the dense trees. The cottage was fully intact. Through the windows, I could see the entire family gathered around their dinner table, chattering away like all was well.

I heaved a sigh and leaned heavily against the nearest tree. *All was well.* I should have known it was, rather than jumping to the worst conclusion I could conjure.

I tended to do that. It was one of things people hated about me.

Frowning, I started to turn from the cottage, only to notice their hearth was silent and empty. But the scent of smoke still pulsed against my senses. Stiffening, I looked around, searching for the source of it. If the smoke wasn't coming from here, then where in fate's damned name was it coming from?

Were my wards finally right? Was someone really out there, camped out in the woods and cooking meat over the flames?

Tensing, I moved through the trees. Twigs snapped underfoot, but the rustle of the wind through the branches hid the sound. I sniffed the air, trying to scent the direction of the smoke. There was something out here that shouldn't be, and I was damn sure I was going to find it.

And then there—a light sound drifted toward me. The steady rise and fall of heavy breathing. I stilled and swivelled my head toward the noise. In the darkness, it took me a moment to understand what I was looking at, but after a time, I saw her. An elven woman was tucked inside a redwood's tree hollow, sleeping.

She wore deep green leathers to blend in with the forest, and her hair was a rich brown that cascaded around her shoulders. Even as curled up as she was, she looked long and lean, like an arrow, and there was something about her that reminded me of the trees. My breath stilled in my lungs as I watched her chest rise and fall once more.

Beside her lay a pack, a bow, and a quiver of arrows. A *weapon*. Of course, she could easily explain that away—she was out hunting for game, I was sure she'd say. She might not be lying if she said that, either.

The ones that hunted me preferred hidden daggers. It was much easier to stab the target in the heart before he had any idea he was in danger.

But there was something about her—the button nose, the high cheekbones, and the line of her sharp jaw. That, combined with her rich brown hair, made it impossible for her to be anyone else. She looked so much like a Rurik.

And if she was who I thought she was, she was here to kill me.

Sorrow weighed heavily on my shoulders. The answer to my dreaded predicament was obvious. The assassin was fast asleep. She'd never see me coming. I could have my axe buried in her skull before she even opened her eyes.

But a vicious ache went through me at the thought of it. I hadn't killed anyone in well over a decade. I'd left that life behind—permanently. It was why I'd come to this island in the first place.

And it was why I planned to stay here for what I wanted to be a very long and boring life. There was enough blood painting my hands. I didn't want any more of it.

What was I to do? What *could* I do? Ignoring her wasn't an option, either. She'd already found me. Soon, she'd nock her arrow, aim it at my head, and send it flying.

Should I take her captive? I could lock her up inside my cottage instead of letting her attempt to kill me, but...then what? I couldn't keep her prisoner forever. And eventually, the villagers would come round—they *always* came round if I went too long without seeing anyone. What the fuck would they think about me keeping an elven woman chained up inside my house?

I scratched the base of my left tusk, thinking. The assassin had found my home tonight, but she hadn't made an attempt on my life yet. I knew how these people worked. Stealth was the highest priority, and staying here any longer than necessary increased the risk that someone might spot her, even out here in the woods.

If she hadn't taken aim yet, there was a reason.

Which meant...she might be after something else—something more than just me. And if she was, I had to find out what it was before she got it.

With a grim nod, I turned away from my new

enemy and wound through the trees in the direction of my cottage. I knew what I needed to do. I would pretend to make friends with the damn elf and get her to trust me.

And if that didn't work? *Then* I'd have no choice but to ask the local blacksmith for some chains.

4

FRIDA

When a soft, wet nose nudged my hand, unrelenting panic lurched through me. I was out of the tree and on my feet with my bow in hand before I saw the creature. A large black cat perched on the leafy ground and gazed up at me with intense black eyes. Her tail curled around her, the fluffy tip sitting on her paws. Her entire body seemed to hum.

"Oh." I laughed awkwardly and lowered my bow. "Hello there, kitty. Sorry, you caught me off guard."

The cat continued to purr. I knelt and reached out a hand. For a long moment, all she did was stare at me, but she eventually rose and padded

35

over. She rubbed her flank against my legs and primly accepted the scratch beneath her chin.

"Good kitty," I said, smiling. "Do you live here? Don't tell me I unknowingly stole your house for the night."

I looked behind me at the tree hollow and its bed of pine needles. It would make a pretty nice den for a cat, I supposed. Some of the cats I'd befriended near my cottage had kept similar dwellings.

"Don't worry. You didn't steal that tree from her. Moira lives with me," a rough, deep voice said.

My entire body went taut. Nerves buzzing, I slowly lifted my gaze to find a towering, muscular orc standing before me with his arms folded over his broad chest. Sunlight filtered in through the canopy and illuminated the silver tusks jutting from his lips and his moss-green skin. He wore his raven hair tied back from his face, revealing the line of rings that decorated his sharply tipped ears. Clad in a simple white tunic with intricate vines embroidered into the neckline, he reminded me of a towering, imposing statue of an infamous warrior —but one someone had placed a flower crown upon. For a moment, I felt flummoxed. I knew I was staring, but I couldn't stop myself.

This *must* be Rune. My mark. My intention to

remain out of sight had vanished into the dawning light. He'd found me—or his cat had.

I cleared my throat and stood, trying to act nonchalant. "Good morning. Sorry, I didn't see you there."

He arched a dark brow, scowling. "That seems unlikely, what with you making camp on my property and all."

I swallowed. "This is your property? It just looked like more of the forest to me…"

"My property line extends out past my cottage and deep into the trees."

"Oh." I shifted on my feet. "I'm sorry. I truly didn't realize. I'll just be on my way…"

This was going horribly. If my father could see me now, he'd be so disappointed. Not one day on the island, and I'd already mucked this up. I just had to hope I could turn it around somehow. Maybe if I vanished into the trees and remained hidden for a while, Rune would forget about me…

I didn't think that was likely, though.

Clenching my jaw, I grabbed my pack from the trunk and started to walk away. Every muscle in my body was so stiff, it was like the wood of the forest had consumed me.

"Wait," Rune called after me.

Dammit.

"It doesn't look like you have much to eat," he said, before I'd even turned back toward him.

I looked over my shoulder, my heart thumping. "I have a bow. I'll hunt."

"Save your arrows," he said. "I've got plenty of food, and I'd love some company. I don't get many visitors out here, you know." A pause. "It's the least you could do after trespassing on my property."

Fuck, fuck, fuck.

Breaking bread with my mark was the last thing I wanted to do. The longer I spent in his presence, the more likely it was he'd remember me when his dragon went missing. And if I made myself too memorable, I'd be forced to take it a step further than I wanted. Guild rules: no witnesses left behind.

Rune's frown deepened when I didn't immediately reply. "Is there some reason why you're reluctant to eat with me? Please tell me it's not because I'm an orc."

"No, no, no," I said quickly. "It's not that. I just…well, I'm feeling a bit out of sorts, I guess. One moment, I'm fast asleep, and the next, a cat is waking me up, and I find out I accidentally camped on someone's property…sorry. It has nothing to do with you being an orc. I'll join you for breakfast. Thank you for the invitation."

Inwardly, I kicked myself. I shouldn't have

agreed. This was a terrible, terrible idea, and yet…I saw no way out of it.

"Good." He smiled, though there was something still tense in his expression. "Follow me, then."

Without further ado, he turned and stalked away. His cat padded after him. My gut churned as I watched Rune's retreating form blend in with the dense foliage. For a brief moment, I considered dashing away while his back was turned to me. If I was quick enough, I could scale a tree and hide in the branches far above. Eventually, he'd forget about me. It would be like I'd never even been here…

The smart thing to do was run. My training told me to run.

Still, I hesitated just a second too long. Rune paused and turned. Through the brush, his gleaming eyes were all I could see. "Aren't you coming?"

Swallowing, I nodded. But he didn't continue forward. He waited there in the brush, his gaze locked on my face, like he suspected I might not follow him if he turned his back to me again. If I tried to run now, what would he do? Would he watch me go or would he follow? The sharp glint in his eyes told me it would *not* be the former.

And so I hefted my pack higher onto my shoulder and followed the orc through the woods.

~

There was no end to the forest when we reached Rune's cottage. The small timber home seemed part of the woods itself. It had even been built with one wall flush against a tree, the branches wending through the wall before sprouting its lush, verdant leaves over the roof. Vines crawled along every wooden beam and trailed across a wide window spilling yellow light onto the forest floor. Wildflowers grew in untamed bunches, and moss-covered stones emerged from the ground, surrounded by elaborately crafted wooden chairs. Nearby, a few wicker baskets were stacked against an outbuilding nearly as large as the cottage, the top one overflowing with mushrooms.

"This is your house?" I asked, not bothering to mask my surprise.

I didn't know what I'd been expecting, but it certainly wasn't this. Rune's name had been etched onto the infamous Assassin's Guild list, which meant he wasn't the sort of person one might wish to find themselves alone with. And even though I'd known he lived in a forest, I'd still imagined a dingy, dark hole full of weapons and dust. Something that outwardly reflected the monster he was within.

But there was life and color here—so much that it felt like the house was alive.

Rune grunted, then hauled open the front door. The aroma of woodsmoke and freshly cooked fish drifted from the house, making my mouth water. My stomach groaned, begging me to forgo all logic and follow Rune inside so I could fill my empty belly. I was awfully hungry after my night spent in the woods.

This was fine. No, it was more than fine. Going inside his house was a *grand* idea. Because befriending him like this could help me with my task.

My assignment was to find the bloody dragon. So far, there'd been no sign of one. Truth be told, I'd expected clear evidence as soon as I'd found Rune. According to legend, dragons ran extremely hot. If they wandered through a forest like this, they'd burn things. It was one of the reasons the crown had considered them so dangerous, back when hundreds of them roamed the world. Just their mere existence was a threat big enough for most people to fear them.

I'd seen no patches of burned bushes in the forest, nor did I see any char on Rune's property.

Just lots and lots of wood, moss, vines, and flowers. Which meant the dragon was clearly hiding somewhere else. Maybe if I got Rune to trust me, he'd share his dragon secrets with me. It might be my best chance of succeeding on this mission.

And if the more likely scenario were true—if Erik was wrong and there were no dragons—well, I'd worry about that later.

By the time I'd solidified the plan in my head, an awkward silence had descended upon us. Rune hovered inside the doorway. He awkwardly cleared his throat, then shook his head and walked into his cottage with thunderous steps. He looked like he was sorely regretting his invitation for me to dine with him.

Squaring my shoulders, I followed Rune inside. The interior of his cottage was hot, and my gaze was instantly drawn to a blazing hearth-fire. Beside it sat an old rocking chair and a table piled with books whose leather covers were worn and curled. Several shelves held piles of books, scrolls, and hand-whittled carvings of wolves and cats.

The forest seemed to force its way inside. Ivy climbed the walls, and clay pots held enormous plants bursting with life. A worktable sat in the far corner, covered in wood pieces and carving instruments. Above it, the walls held dozens of intricate schematics, the ink scribbled onto yellowed parchment to depict homes, tables, and shelves that Rune planned to build—or had already.

The opposite corner held a dining table, where Rune had already laid out breakfast. Bread, butter, eggs, and fish filled wooden platters, along with a wheel of orange cheese. The smell filled the air, along with the unmistakable scent of wood shavings, vellum, and ink.

The sight and scent of it all carved a hole inside me, then filled it with a haunting *ache*. A yearning for a home just like this, rather than the sterile gray walls of the guild.

"You have a lovely cottage," I said, my voice rough. As I shifted on my feet, the floor creaked. "It's beautiful."

"Thank you. Have a seat." Oblivious to the painful ache in my chest, Rune motioned to one of the high-backed chairs. Engravings ran along the wooden back posts. They were unfamiliar to me, but they looked like some kind of lettering. Likely orcish.

Still feeling awkward, I crossed the room, the floorboards creaking beneath my steps, and took a seat. The legs scraped loudly against the floor, and I winced. As if immune to the sound, Rune settled into the chair opposite mine and forked some eggs onto his plate. No one said a bloody word.

"Got some chickens?" I asked, desperate to clear the silence.

Frowning, he looked up to meet my gaze. "Sorry, no. Is chicken a standard breakfast food in…wherever you came from?"

So he knew I wasn't from around here. I'd expected that. On the journey over, Louisa had given me a bit more information about the island. Only a few hundred folk called this place home. A stranger's face stuck out like a sore thumb.

"Um, no. We don't have chickens for breakfast," I answered. "I meant because of the eggs. I saw your mushroom foraging basket outside and thought maybe you had your own chickens, too. For the eggs."

He nodded but didn't say anything. Cheeks burning, I grabbed a slice of bread and buttered it with furious focus. I needed to take a different approach here. If he didn't feel as uncomfortable as I did, I'd eat my shoe. I'd never get him to reveal all his secrets to me unless I could get him to relax. Which meant *I* needed to relax.

Unfortunately, my shoulders felt like stones had taken up residence inside them.

"I'm really curious about your house," I said after a moment.

He sat up a bit straighter. "Oh? How so?"

"Well, I've never seen anything quite like it. It's

almost as if someone built it to be part of the forest."

"Someone *did* build it to be part of the forest," he said gruffly. "That was me."

"You built this place?" I gazed around. The woodworking was incredible. Every beam was slotted perfectly into place, and the wood had been sanded so smoothly that I bet you could slide your palms across them without finding a splinter. But more than that, there was an artistry to it. Several of the beams ended in elaborate carvings. Some had wolf heads, and others had depictions of twisting branches that seemed to reach toward the thatched roof, as if stretching toward the sky beyond. He must have built these chairs, too. And this table. Gods, what a talent.

"It's very nice," I said. "I'm impressed."

The hint of a smile curved his lips. It was the first time he'd done anything but scowl since he'd found me lurking on his property. But the half-smile was gone just as quickly as it had appeared, almost like he'd realized what he was doing and wanted to stop himself.

My stomach twisted. There'd been suspicion in his eyes earlier, too.

Rune didn't trust me, and yet he'd invited me to breakfast. I slowed my chewing. The food was delicious, but what if I'd been too hasty in letting down my guard? I never should have eaten the enemy's food, lest I find it poisoned.

I stabbed a bit of fish with my fork and lifted it toward him. "You don't have any. Want a bite?"

Rune stilled, then levelled his gaze at me across the table. "This might be the first time I've had a visitor offer to feed me, fork to mouth."

My cheeks heated. "Glad to be of service."

For a moment, our gazes locked across the table. There was something dark in his expression, something I couldn't quite read. And I hated that— hated not knowing what he was thinking. What made him tick. When I met someone, I could usually glean the truth of them within a few moments. For example, I'd known Erik was a thieving bastard from the second I'd met him. It was in the twitchy way he moved and the insistence to keep his hands tucked in his pockets, regardless of the situation.

And Erik's eyes held a darkness. Sometimes when I met his gaze, it felt like there was no one in there—like his soul had abandoned him years ago and left the husk of his body behind. Louisa's words of warning echoed in my mind. Maybe she was right. Maybe all the kills he'd notched into his belt over the years had ended up killing something in him, too.

Like Erik, Rune held a darkness, but he didn't

feel empty. He felt...*real*. And I didn't know what to make of that.

"Hand it over, then," he finally murmured, breaking through my charged thoughts.

Heart pounding, I leaned across the table until the fish brushed his lips. With his eyes still locked on mine, Rune opened his mouth and tugged the food off the fork with his teeth, his tusks glinting beneath the flickering hearth-light.

A tidal wave of anticipation consumed me. Every inch of my skin prickled, and heat burned my cheeks. I sat back and lowered my fork to my plate, waiting. After a moment, Rune chewed the food, swallowed, and went back to his eggs.

He didn't twitch. He didn't gasp or fall over dead, which meant he hadn't tried to poison me. Well, that was good.

I should feel relieved, but the churning dread remained. Rune was smiling as he tucked some more food into his mouth, looking far too happy with himself. It was like he knew what I'd been thinking, that I'd suspected the food. And now he thought he'd won this silent, fraught battle of wits.

An unsuspecting person wouldn't be smug about that. Something I'd done must have tipped him off.

That could only mean one thing. Rune had a pretty good idea why I'd come to this island.

5

FRIDA

"So tell me how you came to live on the Floating Forest," I said, after polishing off the rest of the food. My stomach was full now, and the warmth of the cottage had soothed some of my nerves. At the end of the day, I had to embrace my new plan, whether or not Rune suspected me. I'd already fucked up my mission—at least in the way the guild liked to do things.

That didn't mean I'd failed yet. All I had to do was convince Rune I wasn't here for the reasons he thought. He had no evidence against me, nothing but a hunch. I'd just have to prove that hunch wrong.

Rune leaned back in his chair, folding his arms over his chest. "I was about to ask you the same thing."

"Me? But I don't live here."

"You do now, don't you? Most people who come to the Floating Forest are looking for a new life, a new home, and a fresh beginning. I figured you were the same. Otherwise, why'd you end up on this island?"

He was testing me. Rune clearly thought nothing of the sort.

"I only got here last night. I haven't seen enough to know if I want to live here permanently."

He nodded. "But you're considering it?"

"I...well, I suppose so." It seemed like the best excuse.

"Then you're running away from something," he said, his brown eyes sharpening on my face.

I frowned. "That's a leap."

"Is it? Why would a beautiful elf like yourself come here alone if she wasn't running from something in her past? You would have had to leave everything behind. Your home, your friends. Your family."

His words were hitting far too close to home. Years ago, I *had* run from my life and left everything behind. Everything I'd always known. Everyone I'd loved. At the time, I'd been desperate to put as much space between me and my past—my *family's* past—as possible, hoping that I could leave it in the dust. But it had caught up with me in the end.

"You sound like you're speaking from experience," I countered. "Does that mean you were running from something?"

His face clouded over, and the scowl returned. Interesting. I'd been trying to take the attention off me, but I'd landed on a truth he didn't want me to know. Rune *had* fled from something. He was hiding on this island, hoping he'd never get caught. Despite these cozy lodgings, his past held as much darkness as mine did. I was right to suspect there was more to him than met the eye.

Rune heaved a sigh. "I suppose you're right. I did run, same as anyone else who ends up here. I made a mistake once and angered the wrong person. It's haunted me all my life."

I sat back in my chair, my heart pounding. I hadn't expected him to *actually* answer. "What happened?"

"I've said enough already. It's not something I like to talk about," he said gruffly. "Least of all with a stranger."

I pressed my lips together, deciding not to push. At least not yet. If I moved too quickly, those walls of his would raise right back up again.

I cleared my throat. "I get it. I've never talked to anyone about my own…issues."

That, at least, was the truth. No one but my family and the other guild members knew about my desertion and subsequent return. A few of my forest neighbors had asked me about my childhood, my family, and my past, but I'd conjured up lies as explanations. I didn't know how to tell people I'd been born into a family of killers—which meant I was a killer, too. Death swirled in my blood.

Everyone back home—sweet Maella with the flowers in her hair and old Aster who liked to sit on his porch, rocking back and forth and watching the day drift by—weren't like me. If I'd told them the truth, they never would have seen me as anything but an assassin. Someone to avoid at all costs. As it was, they'd been my only friends for so long I hadn't wanted to scare them away. Because of the miles between us, we already went weeks between visits. If the years passed without contact, my unending loneliness would become unbearable.

Of course, that was no longer the case. I had the guild now.

Rune nodded slowly. "I've never told anyone the details about my past, either. Most people here know I've got something that haunts me, but they don't know what it is. I intend to keep it that way."

I cocked my head. "You're being awfully candid

now, for someone who claims he doesn't like to talk."

He waved my words away. "I'd hardly call this candid. All I've told you is that I've got something, but that's hardly surprising. Like I said before, everyone here's running."

I nodded.

"And," he continued, "we're all lucky to have found this place. It's safe from the outside world, or as safe as any place can be. The good folk here don't need to worry about their pasts. They're happy in their bubble, and I intend to make sure it stays that way for a long time to come."

I searched his hawkish gaze. It was easy to understand what he was trying to tell me. Rune wanted me to leave these people alone. And if I didn't, he'd do whatever it took to protect them.

Fine with me. I would never aim my bow at someone who didn't deserve it.

"I've heard that," I said. "About the Isles, I mean. It's one of the safest places in the known world."

"You heard right. Some of the islands don't even allow weapons. We don't have that rule on the Floating Forest, but..." He eyed my bow and quiver of arrows, where I'd stashed them against the wall just beside the door. "I can see the merit in it."

"Don't you have an axe?"

"My axe is for woodworking. If I used it to kill someone, the villagers of Oakwater would banish me from the island. As they should. I don't take lives."

More hidden meanings. More carefully worded threats. I didn't quite understand what I'd done to raise his hackles, but they were as raised as they possibly could be. He was so convinced I'd come here for nefarious reasons that I wouldn't be shocked if he escalated the conversation to outright accusations. Maybe I ought to excuse myself before things went that far. This had been a decent start, as long as we parted on good terms.

"Well, this has been a lovely start to my day." I pushed back my chair and stood. "Thanks again for the breakfast. Would you mind pointing me in the direction of Oakwater? I'm assuming they have a few inns."

He frowned up at me, his lips curling around his tusks. "You're leaving?"

"Yes, I'd like to get settled in somewhere." I kneaded my shoulders with my knuckles, rolling my neck. "I didn't get much sleep last night, camping inside a tree and all. A nap sounds amazing right about now."

A nap did not sound at all amazing. I was far too on edge to fall asleep, nor did I plan to find an inn. I'd camp out in the woods until I'd completed my assignment, making sure none of the other villagers caught sight of my face. But I couldn't tell him that, now could I?

"You should stay," he said quietly.

"I'm sorry?"

"You should stay," he repeated, his voice a little louder this time. "I have a spare room. In exchange, all I ask is for some help with my woodworking. I could really use another pair of hands on some of my builds."

"You want me to stay here. And be your *assistant*?"

He shrugged. "I figure you're new in town, which means you'll need a roof over your head and a job to make some coin. Not sure what better offer you'd get, let alone if you'd get one at all. Oakwater's a small village. And the one inn is routinely full."

I squinted at him. "How's the inn full? I thought you said you didn't get many visitors."

"We don't. People show up, move into the inn, and stay there until they get their homes built, which can take months."

"I see. And you're the one who builds the homes, I'm guessing," I said. "All by yourself?"

"That's why I need another pair of hands."

"I...appreciate the offer."

I didn't know the first thing about woodworking. Sure, I did a bit of carpentry on my cottage when things broke. Once, I'd pulled up a rotting floorboard and replaced it with a new one. I'd sanded the front porch steps after I'd wandered down them barefooted and got a splinter stuck in my toe for days. I'd even built a very small set of shelves, which turned out lopsided and creaky. But that was about the extent of it.

The thing was, this opportunity was *perfect*. Working side by side with him, day after day… living in his house and sharing meals with him. It was the ideal way to convince him I was a lovely, trustworthy elf who he could share his secrets with. And if not, maybe he had some clues hidden around his house, ones that would lead me straight to his dragon.

He'd handed me exactly what I needed to get close to him, plopped on a silver platter. All I had to do was take it.

Which was, incidentally, exactly why I hesitated. With all the suspicions he clearly had about me, he wouldn't make this offer unless he hoped to gain something in return—likely the confirmation he needed to…what, exactly? If he discovered I was part of the guild, what would he do? He said he wasn't a killer, but that was *exactly* the kind of thing a killer would say when they wanted you to trust them.

I'd just have to be careful, that was all. And find what I needed before he did.

"So…" The chair creaked as he shifted his weight on it. "What do you say?"

"All right. I'll take the job." Fate, what was I doing?

Rune's lips quirked. It wasn't quite a smile, but it was better than the furrowed look from a moment before. He held a large, calloused hand across the table. Swallowing, I took it and shook. His skin was shockingly warm, and while his grip was firm, his touch was somehow gentle, too. Heat pooled in my belly.

When he released my hand, I didn't quite know where to look. So I did what any other woman would do when trapped in an awkward situation. I grabbed the cheese and stuffed it into my mouth. As soon as the rich cheddar hit my tongue, all thoughts of Rune's suspicions fled my mind. I nearly moaned from how delicious it was.

Rune watched me silently as I chewed. When I was finished, he cut off another chunk of cheese and dropped it onto my plate.

"Good, eh? It's local," he said.

"Don't tell me you have cows, too? And you make cheese? What, exactly, *can't* you do?"

"Oh, I can do a great many things. Cheese-making isn't one of them, though. That cheddar is from one of the farmers down the road. A family of dwarves. Good folk."

"Ah." I nodded. That must be the family whose house I'd stumbled upon when I'd first arrived. "Well, next time you see them, be sure to tell them their cheese is to die for."

"You can tell them yourself, once you're done eating. I need to pay them a visit about a job, and as my new assistant, I need you to come along."

I slid my eyes down to my plate, then poked at the cheese with my fork. Suddenly, I no longer had much of an appetite, even for the cheese. When I'd agreed to take the assistant position, I'd imagined I could keep myself well hidden from the townspeople. I could hole up, building whatever needed building. Rune didn't strike me as the sociable type, either, so I didn't expect he got many visitors or dinner guests.

I didn't want to make much of a mark here. If anyone figured out who and what I was, it would put them in danger. The guild didn't much like witnesses. Their names tended to end up on the list, even if they were innocents. I'd asked my father about it a few times. Surely, if we only took out those with darkness in their hearts, we should give witnesses a little grace.

But he'd told me we must do whatever it took to protect the guild. If a witness reported us to the authorities, the guild could crumble. We could be taken captive, executed. And then who would be left to remove evil from the world?

It was a solid argument. One I didn't agree with, but that hardly mattered in the end. I wasn't the one in charge. And if someone here—or a lot of someones—ended up on the wrong side of the guild, they'd also end up without a head.

I blew out a breath. "Do you need me to go with you? I'm awfully tired, like I said before."

"Consider it your induction." He stood from the table and grabbed some parchment and a quill from the woodworking corner of his house. "You can take notes."

Without further ado, he walked to the door, yanked it open, and motioned me outside. Swallowing around the lump in my throat, I grabbed the chunk of cheese—for emotional support—and followed him to the home of the dwarves.

6

FRIDA

A tense silence saturated the air between us as we walked from Rune's property to the home of the dwarves. On our way out the door, I'd thrown my cloak around my shoulders to drown my face in the shadows of the hood. I knew it would make little difference, though. When we met the dwarves, I couldn't lurk behind Rune, refusing to reveal myself. Doing so would bring far more attention to me than if I acted like a normal person with nothing to hide.

As twigs crunched underfoot, I tossed back the hood. Sweat claimed strands of my hair, plastering them to my forehead. Even with the dense canopy overhead, the sun cast an insistent heat upon us. In the distance, the soft rush of waves pushed through the trees, tempting me to abandon this ridiculous plan and dive into the cooling sea instead.

But I'd committed. There really was no turning back now.

As soon as we stepped off the path, an entire estate sprawled across a verdant field cut into the heart of the forest. A handful of buildings were scattered throughout the clearing, along with the home I'd stumbled upon last night. Several resembled the outbuilding I'd seen back at Rune's, but a stable, a granary, and a cattle barn added to the collection. Several horses, their manes slick and gleaming black, swivelled their heads our way and nickered, toeing the ground. At the sight of them, my heart ached. I wished Stella was here.

A dwarf bustled out from the granary's open doors, a shovel hanging from his hand. His long ginger hair flowed around his broad shoulders, and bells jingled where they were woven through his curly beard. Damp dirt stained the knees of his coveralls, and his boots were caked in mud, grains, and hay.

He smiled as he bustled over to us, though it came across as more of a grimace than a grin. In fact, as he drew closer, I noticed the purple bags that clung to the bottom of his eyes, too. "Rune! Fate, I'm glad to see you."

I looked up to see Rune frown. "What's the matter, Arvid? You look like shit."

"Tactful as always, thank you." Arvid's smile lightened a bit for the smallest of moments, but then vanished when he reached us. He drove the shovel into the ground, leaned one arm on top of the handle, and sighed heavily. "We nearly lost Bertha."

Rune's body seemed to *expand*. He straightened, his eyes alert as he cast his gaze around the farm, clearly searching for whoever this Bertha was. "What do you mean?"

Arvid tightened his grip on the shovel. "I mean exactly what I said. Mellor and I left her out grazing yesterday morning while we were tending to the horses. I only had my back turned to her for a half hour at most. I think that's the only reason we managed to find her—she wasn't gone too long. She ended up on the bloody beach for some fate-damned reason."

"Well, I know you must have been worried sick, but it sounds like it all worked out," Rune said. "Why'd you call me over?"

"We need a fence, Rune. We've already lost two cows. Can't afford to lose any more. Or any of the chickens and horses and sheep." Arvid looked grim. "We should have put up a fence ages ago, and it can't wait any longer now."

"A fence." Rune scratched the base of one of his tusks, nodded, and looked around. "It's doable, but it's going to take some time, what with the house build going on right now. We'll have to split our time between here and there. Think you can hold down the fort for a couple of weeks while we work on it?"

"*We?*" Arvid arched a brow, then glanced at me. A startled look crossed his face, like he'd only just now noticed me here. "Who's this, then?"

"This is my new assistant," Rune said gruffly. "Her name is…"

"Frida," I supplied.

"Well, it's about damn time," Arvid said with an approving nod. He relinquished his tight hold on the shovel and padded around Rune's side to peer at me. "Well, don't be shy. Come closer. Let's have a look at ya."

I stepped out of Rune's shadow and into the sun. Arvid beamed up at me. "Well, aren't you a pretty elven lass? I was going to ask how you convinced old grump here to give you a job, but now I see."

My cheeks heated. "No, it's not like that. He's just…being kind, that's all."

That or he was trying to trick me into revealing who I was. Most likely, it was the latter. He suspected me, that much was clear.

"Hmm," Arvid said with a little laugh, then turned his attention back to Rune. "We can manage for two weeks. What'll it cost us?"

"Frida?" Rune asked, looking expectantly at me.

"I'm sorry, what?" I asked, thinking I'd missed a sentence or two.

"Arvid asked the price of the fence."

"Right…" I lifted the parchment he'd handed me, but there was nothing written on it. He'd only given it to me for taking notes, he'd said. So why was he asking me a question? "I'm sorry, did you mention pricing before we came here?"

"I'm letting you take the reins on the fence, so you get to decide the pricing," he said.

I understood what he was doing. Did he think I'd been born yesterday? Never in a million years would he have handed an entire build over to a new apprentice on her first day. Not unless he had ulterior motives.

Rune wanted to keep me distracted. If I was swamped with work, building this fence, I wouldn't have time to hunt down his dragon.

He was clever, I'd give him that. Just not clever enough to trick me.

"I couldn't possibly," I said, casting my eyes to the ground as if in supplication. "Not on my first day. I'm nowhere near ready."

"Oh, don't sell yourself short. I know how eager

you must be to really dig into something," Rune said. "Consider it your 'induction' task."

I tensed, my eyes flying up to his face. His expression betrayed nothing, but there'd been a bite to his words—a *knowing*. It was almost like he wanted me to know that he knew, or at least make me worry that he knew. And if I insisted on turning down this offer, it would be like admitting my guilt.

With a tight smile, I said, "How could I say no to that?"

"Good. So the price?" Rune prodded.

My gaze was once again drawn to Arvid, and there was hope gleaming in his eyes.

"Five wheels of your best cheese," I said.

His eyes brightened, and a full smile spread across his face. Something akin to fondness stirred in my chest, even though I'd just met the man. "You'd build an entire fence around my farm for five wheels of cheese?"

"For your cheese, I'd do nearly anything," I said with a smile. "It's probably the best I've ever tried."

"Ha!" He stuck out a calloused hand. "It's a deal, then."

We shook on the offer, then he showed me around his farm so I could get a better sense of how much material we needed. I made some notes and asked how tall he wanted it. All the while, Rune trailed behind us, listening to our conversation like the mentor he was pretending to be.

When I'd gotten what I felt like was enough information, Rune and I said our goodbyes and returned to his cottage with three wheels of cheese as a down-payment tucked into my cloak, which I'd turned into a makeshift sack that I'd tossed over my shoulder.

I had so many questions I wanted to ask Rune, but not a single one of them felt safe. But I refused to spend the return walk in utter silence again, so I settled on the only question I could think of that didn't feel like an invitation for accusations.

"He mentioned a couple of other cows. What happened to them?" I asked.

Rune frowned. "We're not quite sure. I helped Arvid search the woods after they went missing, but we never saw hide nor hair of them."

"How long ago was it?"

"Two weeks. Maybe three."

"Well, surely cows can't just up and disappear. They must be out there still."

He nodded. "That's what I thought, too. But I helped them scour these woods for days. 'Course you're welcome to try yourself if you think you can do better."

Out of the corner of my eye, I tried to examine his face. He was nearly unreadable, though. The muscles around his jaw were tight, but they always seemed to be. Grouchiness, I was quickly learning, was his default. Still, I couldn't help but wonder if the tension was at least partially due to something else.

Something like...he knew where the cows went. Straight into the mouth of his dragon.

"Arvid and his family," I said after a moment. "Are they close friends of yours?"

"I can't say I have any close friends," came his —unsurprisingly—gruff answer. But after a brief moment, he added, "They're good folk. I suppose out of everyone on this island, I'm closest to them." He grunted a chuckle. "Sounds a bit sad when you put it like that."

"Well, I know how you feel," I found myself saying. "Back home, my closest neighbors lived well over a mile away, so I spent most days never seeing another friendly face. Not unless you count my horse, which I very much do. Her name is Stella."

"Back home? And where is that exactly? You never said."

I pursed my lips, considering the many lies I could choose. But then I figured I ought to go with the truth—or as close to the truth as I could get. He could clearly see I was elven. He could likely hear it in my accent, too. "The Kingdom of Edda. I lived in the forest just north of the city of Vilmar."

"Hmm. All by yourself?"

"Yeah," I said softly. "All by myself."

A look of suspicion crossed his face, quick as lightning. That told me two things. One, he didn't believe a damn word I said. Two, he knew how the guild operated. He knew we didn't live alone in forest cottages, surrounded by the scent of fresh wildflowers and the orchestra of morning birdsong. The number of people who knew our lodging situation could be contained on a single sheet of parchment. Ordinary folk—those outside of the guild—weren't privy to that kind of information. I hadn't even known my family had moved into the guild-hall—or that a guild-hall even existed—until I'd told my brother I'd join.

I'd then had to swear a vow to the Old Gods that I would abstain from all manner of enjoyable activities. Only then could I know the guild's secrets.

For a very long time, I'd had no idea where my family was. Just that they lived inside the city.

"Why'd you leave it?" Rune asked when we reached his cottage.

I stared at the cat perched in the window, basking in the midday sun. It was such a sweet sight it made my heart ache. "I suppose I was lonely."

An honest answer—perhaps more honest than I'd intended to be with Rune. Because while I wanted to rip down his walls so I could reveal his every secret, I didn't want him to tear down mine.

Rune searched my face with eyes less angry than they'd been a moment before. "Why not just go to the city?"

"Not enough plants for my liking," I said, then cleared my throat. Time to steer this conversation in a different direction. "So, if I build the entire fence myself, do I get to eat all this cheese? Because otherwise, I probably should have asked for more of it."

Rune actually cracked a smile.

7

RUNE

I led Frida toward my workshop, trying not to let my expression betray my mess of a brain. All morning, I'd been laying traps. So far, she'd dodged every damn one. I'd expected her to turn down the job of building the fence for the dwarves. It locked her in for two weeks. Wouldn't she want to finish her guild assignment before then? And when I'd asked her about home, I thought she'd make up some story, like she'd grown up in the orc city of Fafnir or something. And since her accent was so strongly elvish, it'd be clear she was lying.

She'd been truthful about her home city, though.

A seed of doubt had taken root inside my mind. I wanted to rip it up and throw it to the birds, but I also didn't want to treat her like an assassin if she wasn't one. I might be a gruff bastard, but I wasn't a monster.

Because, if her story *was* true, she needed my help. She needed a job and a home and food.

As I shoved open my workshop door, I nodded to myself. I needed to find a way to confirm who she was. For now, I'd show her how to build a fucking fence and hope to fate that I could get her to warm to this place in case she was here for something else.

"Here we are." I tugged open the curtains to let in the sun. The midday light washed the shop in shades of yellow, illuminating the motes of sawdust drifting through the room like woody snowflakes. I scratched my tusk, suddenly aware of the jumble of mess that cluttered the space. I wished I'd thought to tidy up in here before showing Frida.

Not that it mattered to me what she thought. I just hadn't had any visitors inside my shop in... well, I couldn't remember the last time someone had been in this shed except for me.

Frida deposited her sack of cheese on the floor and clasped her hands beneath her chin, gazing around the room with...adoration? That couldn't be right.

"I thought your workspace inside the house

was incredible, but this...this is something else!" Her eyes sparkled as she took it all in.

"It is?" I asked, suspicious. It was just an old workshop, one cluttered with too many hammers, nails, and scraps of wood.

She gingerly stepped through the mess, making her way to the far wall, where I'd tacked up an assortment of sketches and designs for the towns-folk cottages. She motioned at one I'd added a bit of color to, the home I'd built for a group of travelling minstrels who'd arrived here three years ago. It was a large, sprawling estate with at least a dozen rooms. It had taken me thirteen months from start to finish, but the looks on their faces when they'd first walked inside had been well worth the effort.

"May I?" She looked over her shoulder at me, and as much as I tried to find some insincerity in her expression, I couldn't. I nodded my acqui-escence.

She reached out as if to pluck the parchment from the wall, but then she paused before letting her hand drop back to her side. "This is beautiful. Is it just something you drew on a whim? Or did you see it somewhere?"

"That's one of my builds," I said gruffly.

She twisted back toward me. "You built this house? By yourself?"

"I had some help carrying some supplies to the site, but…for the most part, yes."

For a moment, she just stared at me. So I stared right back, trying to get the measure of her. Trying to read the thoughts hovering just behind her eyes. And as we stood there, on opposite sides of my shop, I had the sudden urge to just ask. Maybe it would be best to get it all out in the open. Of course, if she *was* an assassin, it wasn't like she'd admit it. And then I'd lose any cards I held.

Before I could make up my mind, she broke the heavy silence. "I'm afraid my pitiful fence won't measure up to what I'm sure the dwarves expect from you."

I held out a hand. "Let's see what you've got."

She flicked her eyes down to the parchment, nibbling on her bottom lip. "Honestly, I'm not very good at sketching."

"Just let me see it," I said.

Cringing, she passed the parchment over my worktable. She'd taken a fine set of notes, but she wasn't wrong about her sketch. All wonky lines and crooked angles, it looked like a child had drawn it, though I didn't have the heart to tell her that. Still, I couldn't help a little ribbing.

"I think you handed me the wrong parchment," I said dryly.

"What?" Frowning, she looked at her empty

hands, like another sheet might suddenly materialize there. "But that's the only one I have."

"Well, you see…" I held up her drawing. "This is a sketch of a horse, not a fence."

A furious blush filled her cheeks. "That does *not* look like a horse."

"Doesn't much look like a fence, either." I grinned.

She propped her fisted hands on her hips, wrinkling her nose. For a brief—very brief, in fact— moment, my breath caught. Fate, she looked nothing like an assassin half the time. All the ones I'd met over the years, including her father, had hardened edges sharpened by every kill they notched into their belt. My eyes were drawn to her waist and the leather belt that encircled it. No notches there. Nice hips, though, I couldn't help but notice. As long and lean as she was, the lass had curves.

She sighed, drawing my attention back to her face. "It's really terrible, isn't it? I mean, look at your sketch here, then look at mine."

"Really, it's not so bad," I found myself saying. "It's like any other talent. You just need some practice, that's all. For example, what would you say you're good at?"

"Archery and horse-riding," she said without a hint of hesitation.

I nodded. "And could you hit a bullseye the first time you nocked an arrow?"

"Honestly, I don't remember a time I've ever missed," she said. In another situation, those words would come across as the epitome of bragging, but there was something so matter-of-fact in the way she said it, like she was commenting on the color of the sky and nothing more. Confidence. I liked that in a woman.

"Well, if that's the case, it's a shame we can't build a home by shooting arrows at a bullseye," I said, laughing.

Frida stood up a little straighter, and the hint of a smile twitched on her lips.

"What?" I asked.

"Nothing." But she looked genuinely delighted, though I couldn't fathom by what.

I shook my head. "Shall we get started?"

"Sure. How do we begin?" She hopped on the table, her legs dangling over the edge. Peering up at me with big brown eyes, she struck me once again as the antithesis of the guild members I'd once known. There was something bright in her expression—a kind of eagerness and exuberance that betrayed the guild's rules. Outward displays of happiness were highly frowned upon, as were all manner of enjoyable things: drinking mead, laughing uproariously with friends, engaging in intimacy…

If she was a member of the guild, she'd have taken a vow of celibacy. *And* sobriety.

An idea sparked to mind. There might be a quicker way to confirm who and what she was. And as tempting as it was to lean in and try to kiss her now—just to go ahead and get it done—I wouldn't take things that far. I was an orc with monstrous tusks. She wouldn't want to kiss me, even if she *wasn't* part of the guild.

"I'll help you out with the sketch, then we'll take the afternoon off," I said, carefully watching her face. "I don't usually work Freyasday anyway. The local minstrels play an entire set at the tavern, and the whole village usually turns out for it."

Something flashed in her eyes, but it was gone just as quickly as it had appeared. "Oh. Right. And you normally go to this minstrel evening, do you?"

I arched a brow. "Why wouldn't I?"

"You said yourself you don't have a lot of friends."

"Don't see what that has to do with sitting in a tavern, enjoying some songs and some ale," I muttered, though I knew she had me there. I *had* told her I didn't have friends. Should have kept that fucking morsel of information to myself.

"So you just sit in the tavern alone," she said skeptically.

"What does it matter if I do?" My frown deepened. "We're going to the tavern later, and you're going to like it."

She blinked and sat up a little straighter, where she still perched on my worktable. "Já já, Captain."

I squinted at her. "You're not going to argue with me?"

She shrugged. "Didn't want to give you an excuse to toss me over your shoulder and carry me there, kicking and screaming."

The mental image flashed in my mind, and a strange tug went through me as I pictured her long brown hair tumbling over her shoulders while she gripped me, squealing. I blinked, shaking away those thoughts. Frida was a gorgeous lass, but I couldn't let myself forget—even for a moment—who she might be.

Tonight, I would find out the truth about her. If she was a member of the Assassin's Guild, she'd beg off the ale. She'd refuse to dance. She'd never allow me to flirt with her. And then I could relax— or find a way to trap her here.

8

FRIDA

After Rune sketched a new version of the fence, he showed me to the room where I'd 'live' for the foreseeable future. The shuttered windows were flung wide, and the midday sun cast the timber floor in yellow. A small bed with a straw mattress was tucked into the corner, where a towel had been set on the patchwork quilt.

An oil lamp perched on the bedside table, along with a stack of leather-bound books, covers worn and faded, as if they'd been loved well. The ivy from the main room spilled through the cracks in the walls here, too. Some sprouted purple buds, emitting a sweet scent that made my bones hum with a sense of…*right*.

For a moment, I stood there in the middle of the

room with my eyes closed and head tipped back. I breathed it all in, letting the scents of the wilderness wash over me and banish the tension in my body. Despite everything—despite being trapped in a house with a mark who had a handsome face and a toe-curling laugh—at least I had the forest. If it all became too much to bear, I could walk outside and get lost in the trees for a while. I could run and hide in the uppermost branches, waiting for Louisa's ship to return so I could sail away from this mess.

Of course, that would mean returning to the city of Vilmar and all that went with it. The guild and its suffocating walls, Erik's demands, my father's disappointment. I sat hard on the mattress, feeling lost. I didn't know how I was going to do what I'd come here to do. And if I didn't do it, I had no idea how I'd face going back.

Sighing, I opened my pack and unloaded all my belongings. There wasn't much that would be useful here. Just a few changes of clothes, a waterskin, some arrowheads, a comb, and my bedroll. I tucked it all away in a single drawer, though I left the bedroll and waterskin in my pack, along with a few strips of jerky, just in case I needed to get out of here fast.

A soft knock sounded on the door. "Frida? Do you need anything? I wasn't sure if you wanted to bathe before we headed into the village..."

I perked up a bit at that. After wearing my cloak out in the heat, my leathers were sticking to my skin, and I hadn't given my hair a good wash in days. I crossed the room and pulled open the door. Rune hovered on the other side of it, fisted hand raised, like he was readying himself to knock again. He cleared his throat, and his hand dropped to his side.

"Sorry, I wasn't sure if you heard me," he said.

"I would love a bath," I said brightly.

"I don't have one," he said regretfully, "but there's a waterfall a short walk away. We've got time, if you want to use it."

"Sure, that'd be great, thanks." And perhaps I could get a few moments alone to poke around the woods for dragon evidence.

Rune waited by the door while I grabbed the towel and a change of clothes—a simple linen tunic dyed a dark green and a pair of brown trousers. I didn't have anything nicer. When I'd packed, it wasn't like I'd expected to spend an evening drinking and dancing...which would be tough to navigate. I'd vowed to abstain from both those things, not that I agreed with the guild about it. Still, I'd made the vow, and I knew my father would expect me to keep it.

Nevermind. I'd worry about it later. I padded out the door and followed Rune outside. I expected him to point me in the general direction of the falls so that I could have a few moments alone. But no, he started walking down the path right by my side.

"I'm sure I can find my way," I said, pointing ahead. "It's just down this path, I'm guessing?"

"I'd hate for you to get lost on your first day," he said gruffly.

I frowned. "Honestly. I'm not as hopeless as you think I am."

"Oh, I don't think you're hopeless at all, Frida." His lips quirked. "Except when it comes to drawing a fence."

Without thinking, I swatted his arm. And as soon as my fingers grazed his warm skin, brushing across his taut biceps, everything in me tensed. I yanked back my hand, my cheeks heating. His eyes darted to my waist, then to my hand. His expression was intensely unreadable, and I couldn't tell if he was annoyed I'd touched him or if he was just surprised.

I tried to pretend like nothing had happened. "It's not my fault you can't recognize true talent when you see it. That fence I drew? It's art."

He chuckled again—that low, delicious sound I'd heard back in the workshop. It had caught me off guard then, and it caught me off guard now, too. His smiles were as intermittent as the clouds on this clear sky day, and laughter was even more of a rarity. It was such a lovely sound.

"I'll make sure to hang it in a place of honor back at the house," he said. "It can go near the hearth, where everyone who visits can see it."

"Above the hearth. Where it will most likely catch fire."

That chuckle rumbled in his chest again. "Can't say I'd be sorry to see it go up in flames."

I shook my head, annoyed but amused at the same time. Because I couldn't pretend like I didn't want to throw the sketch into the fire myself. An oddly companionable silence descended upon us as we navigated the path. Soon the rush of falling water drowned out the sounds of the birds, insects, and critters scurrying across the fallen leaves.

A clearing yawned before us, sunlight streaming in through a break in the canopy. I slowed to a stop and gasped. A sheet of crystal water poured over the side of a small cliff, though it was more of a ledge that cut into the side of a gently sloping hill. The water frothed where the falls hit the pond, but it was so still and peaceful— and such a brilliant gleaming blue—beyond it. Tufts of wildflowers were scattered along the edge, their yellow bulbs reflected along the surface.

"Absolutely incredible," I breathed.

I felt Rune's eyes on my face, so I turned to look

up at him. He was studying me, again with that esoteric expression.

"What?" I asked him.

"Do you always do that? Every time you see something?"

I searched his gaze. "I don't know what you mean."

"You seem to find wonder in everything. The dwarves' farm, my workshop, this waterfall."

"That's because there *is* a lot of wonder in it." I shrugged. "It's so beautiful compared to the city."

He stilled. "I thought you said you lived in a cottage in the woods."

Fuck. I'd let that one slip out, too distracted by the charm of this place.

"I was just answering your question. You asked me if I find beauty in everything, and I don't. The city is so drab and dull to me. That's why I didn't live there."

I needed to put an end to this conversation before I let something else slip. Best way to do that? The ultimate distraction. So I started peeling off my leathers, right there in front of him.

Rune saw at once what I was doing. With an awkward throat clear, he turned and put his back to me. "You could have given me a warning."

"What's the problem?" I asked as I tossed my

arm bracer to the ground. "You've never seen a naked woman before?"

"Of course I have. I'm normally the one doing the clothes-removal, though."

"Turn around and help me then," I said with a grin.

"I'm sorry?"

"You heard me."

Rune shifted on his feet. "You're asking me to undress you?"

I laughed, toeing off my boots. "I'm just messing with you, Rune."

Except…looking at the taut muscles of his back, visible even beneath his cream tunic, I didn't think him throwing me around would be an entirely unpleasant experience. I hadn't been intimate with many people. Over the years, there'd been one elven man and a couple of women—both humans—but none of them had ever sparked a fire in me the way I'd always yearned for. Enjoyable? Sure. Passionate and romantic? Eh.

When I was younger, I dreamed of meeting someone who would sweep me off my feet and stand beside me in the middle of a storm. Who'd walk with me even into the darkest of places. Who'd do absolutely *anything* just to see me smile. Now that I was older, I worried love like that didn't exist. That the romance stories I'd read could only ever be fictional.

A moment of silence passed between us before Rune asked, "Is this payback for what I said about your sketch?"

A shot of laughter tore from my throat. "No, payback would be shoving you into the pond fully clothed. So maybe I should do just that." But as soon as I'd said it, my laughter died and a lump of hot coal sat heavily on my chest. "Oh. I'm so sorry. I wasn't thinking. I didn't mean…"

He turned his head, just slightly, so he still didn't see me half-dressed. "It's all right. Most people forget, since it's not something most have to worry about."

Orcs were born with a skin condition that caused sensitivity to fresh water. They were severely allergic, and it formed angry welts. Rain and lake water like this could cause it, though salt seemed to dull the issue. Back in Fafnir, the city of the orcs, the clouds only rained salt water. I'd only met a few orcs over the years, but they all had this condition. Most didn't like to talk about it. I'd really put my foot in my mouth this time.

"I really am sorry," I said.

"Don't be." He shrugged, then a wry grin spread across his face. "It's what I am. Just like a 'terrible artist' is what you are."

My mouth dropped open, and I swept the towel from the ground and threw it at his back. It hit him with a soft *hiss*, then gently tumbled to the ground again.

"Careful," he warned. "Two can play at this game. Keep that up, and I'll leave you here to fend for yourself *without* the damn towel."

"Nope, you're just bluffing. The last thing you want to do is leave me unattended."

"And why is that, Frida, hmm?"

I didn't answer. We were beginning to tiptoe too close to a subject I wanted to avoid—me, why I was here, and why he was suspicious of me. So I quietly removed the rest of my clothes, walked across the soft grass, and eased over the lip of the pond. As soon as the cool water enveloped my aching body, a hiss of relief spilled from my lips. I might have even moaned.

"That good, eh?" Rune asked. He'd returned to standing with his back very resolutely turned toward me, facing the direction we'd come. His powerful form was backlit by the sun, enhancing the shape of his broad shoulders. I found myself staring at him, and started to look away—but then didn't. He couldn't see me. He'd never have to know I was enjoying the view.

"Are you really going to stand there the whole time I'm bathing?" I asked.

"You'll be done soon, won't you? Might as well wait."

He really wasn't going to go away. All day, he'd left me alone for no more than a moment or two at a time. It was clear he was keeping an eye on me, likely to make sure I didn't unearth the secrets he'd buried around this island.

An idea sprouted in my mind. Perhaps if he got a little sloshed tonight, he'd sleep like a fallen redwood log and I could sneak out of the house to investigate. It meant another night of too-little-rest, but this was what I'd come here for. It wasn't a holiday.

After I'd washed my hair and scrubbed my skin with the bar of soap Rune had given me, I hauled myself up and over the lip of the pond. Water cascaded down my chest, leaving droplets glistening on the verdant grass. Rune waited silently as I towelled off, and tension practically thrummed in his body. A fist clenched by his side, and his back muscles looked even more taut than they had before.

I glanced around, wondering what had set him off. Was the dragon lurking nearby? Was he worried I'd spot the beast?

"Do you hear that?" I asked, wringing my hair with the towel.

"You dripping everywhere? Yes."

"No, it's a rustling noise, like something's out there in the forest. Something big."

I held my breath, waiting for a reaction. He turned toward me, frowning. And then his gaze landed on my chest. I sucked in a breath, heat flooding my face and neck. The warm humid air still caressed my bare skin, peaking my nipples. My very bare nipples. I'd yet to dress, and I had the towel wrapped around my hair.

"Shit. Fuck." But he didn't turn. He stood there —as if frozen—for a long, fraught moment, his eyes locked on my breasts, before clearing his throat. He swallowed, then cast his eyes to the ground. "I wasn't thinking. I shouldn't have looked. Sorry."

"I don't mind. It's just some skin." But my whole body felt feverish. I was even sweating a little again, and I'd only just climbed out of the pond. Quickly, I finished drying my hair and threw on the clothes I'd brought with me. To be certain, I checked my breasts were covered, and then I cleared my throat. "I'm done now."

He lifted his gaze. There was a flush to his cheeks. "I suppose we should make our way to Oakwater now."

Nothing in his voice held a hint of excitement for the evening.

"Are you sure you still want to go?" I asked.

A curious expression stole across his face. Then

he nodded firmly. "Absolutely. This is your first night on the Floating Forest. We need to make it a memorable one for you."

"Technically, it's my second night. I spent my first one inside a tree." I smiled.

"All the more reason to make this one as good as it can be," he replied.

"If I'm being honest, I didn't mind the tree. It was quite cozy in there."

"Hmm." He held out his arm, so I could slide my hand into the crook of his elbow. "*If* you're being honest? Now, tell me, Frida, why wouldn't you be?"

"No reason, Rune." I tucked my hand into his arm. "No reason at all."

I swore the sky rumbled in response, like the Old God of Thunder heard my lie and wanted to strike me down with the most painful bolt of lightning. And if I *was* being honest, I would say I'd probably deserve it.

9

FRIDA

Oakwater was a bustling little village, its inhabitants lit up in the orange glow of the evening sun. Rune led me along a dirt street that was churned up by wagon wheels. The timber buildings were packed in close, where a clearing had formed due to a natural break in the trees. But a few towering redwoods still stood tall and proud amongst the homes. A group of laughing pixies clustered on a blanket in the shade of the tallest one. Their multi-colored wings matched the flowers.

We continued past them and moved onward down a row of shops. The signs pronounced the wares they sold: books and ink, alchemist supplies, or breads and cakes. Among them was a blacksmith shop and a fishmonger, too. And at the end of the row stood the tavern.

The doors were flung wide, spilling song and laughter into the street. Several patrons were clustered on the benches outside, where their tables were already full of tankards. I followed Rune through the door and into the humid warmth. The place was already packed, throngs of patrons facing the stage at the far end of the rectangular room. Timber beams lined the ceiling above. Decorations dangled from them: acorns and dried flowers and pine cones.

The minstrels were already in full swing. An elven woman perched on a stool, plucking at her lute, while a pixie sang along, her black curly hair bouncing along with the thud of her foot. Two others had taken the stage with them. One was on drums. He was a tall shadow demon—nearly as tall as Rune—and his gaze was sharp as he scanned the crowd, like he was hunting the room for someone. The look in his eye unnerved me, and there was something oddly familiar about him. A moment of panic clutched my heart and squeezed. Could he somehow be here to watch my every move? But then that hawkish gaze passed right over me, like I was no more important to him than anyone else. It was just my paranoia getting to me.

The fourth member of their little team was,

from what I could tell, a human. With sun-kissed skin and soft brown eyes, she stood off to the side playing the harp, like she didn't want to take any of the spotlight herself. But the sound of her playing brought mist to my eyes. I clasped my hands before me, awe filling my chest.

"Ah, there you go again. Let me guess, you think all this is the most beautiful thing you've ever laid eyes on," Rune said a little gruffly, though there was a hint of fondness there, too.

"It is quite beautiful," I said softly.

He looked a little pleased by that. "Well, find us somewhere to sit. I'll grab us two ales."

Before turning to go, he arched a brow, almost like he suspected an objection to his offer. An assassin who'd made a vow to the guild would say no. So obviously I had to do the very opposite of that, even if it might get me in trouble if the guild found out.

"Thank you!" I beamed and wandered off through the crowd. Rune was trying to lay a trap for me again. Little did he know, he'd laid the trap for himself—and he'd stepped squarely into it. My suspicions were confirmed. Rune knew far more about the guild than an ordinary person would, which begged the question…how? Had Rune once been a member of the guild? If so, why had I never heard of him?

And if he was a former member, was that why he'd ended up on Erik's list?

I found the idea troubling. So troubling, in fact, that I bumped into someone's chair because I was too distracted by my thoughts to look where I was going. My stomach collided into it. A bright, hot pain lurched through me, stealing all the breath from my lungs. I stumbled back, but the press of bodies closed in around me, forcing me to remain where I was—trapped between a wall of bodies and the press of the chair.

Black spots darted through my vision. I reached out and timidly tapped the shoulder before me. The owner of said shoulder was a fire demon, whose curving red horns shone wickedly even in the dim lighting of the tavern. He jerked his head sideways, looking back at me.

"Hi, sorry. Do you think you could scoot forward just a tad? I'm a bit stuck here," I said.

He squinted at me. "Are you new here?"

"Yes," I said through gritted teeth. I was struggling to get out the words, what with the way the chair was still smashed into my stomach. Fate, I could hardly breathe.

As if suddenly understanding my predicament, the fire demon dragged his chair an inch forward. It was enough to release me from the suffocating trap. I pulled in a breath of air and squeezed through the gap before settling into one of the empty chairs opposite his.

"Thanks," I said, pressing a hand to my stomach. "There's a lot of folk in here."

"Most of the village. It's pretty boring and quiet around here, so when something happens, we all flock to it." He smiled and stuck out his hand. "I suppose I should welcome you to our little slice of paradise. Name's Valdar."

"I'm Frida." I shook his hand, noting his fingers were covered in ink stains. "Are you a writer?"

"I sure am. If you saw the bookshop down the road, it's mine."

"You got any novels by Silva Sweetwater? I'm a big fan."

"Did you say you're a big fan of *Silva Sweetwater*?" Rune said as he thundered up behind us. He deposited a frothing tankard on the table before me, then took the last remaining seat at the table. His brow was arched in a very exaggerated fashion.

I fought the blush heating my cheeks. "You've heard of her books? I didn't think you were the target audience."

Rune grinned. "I'm not. I didn't think you would be, either. They're quite raunchy, I hear."

"And you don't think a woman can enjoy a nice raunchy book now and again?"

Rune grunted and hoisted his tankard into his hand. I could have sworn a hint of pink dusted his moss-green cheeks. "'Course she can. I just thought..."

"You thought what?" I prodded.

"Nevermind all that. Enjoy your ale," he said.

Rune scratched the bottom of his tusk, frowning. My reading Silva Sweetwater went against everything he thought he knew about members of the Assassin's Guild, something I hadn't even considered. I should have brought it up at his cottage when I'd spotted all the books lying around. With every passing moment, he was becoming more and more convinced he had me wrong.

I lifted my tankard and angled it his way, then tipped the contents down my throat. The ale had a bitter edge to it, but it went down easy, sending a soothing warmth through my belly. As the minstrels broke out into an upbeat song, I gazed around the booming tavern, taking it all in. Everyone looked happy. Content. For a while, I just sat there, relishing it. Letting the happiness wash over me, filling my aching heart with the first moment of peace I'd truly felt since leaving Louisa's ship. Rune sat beside me, doing the same.

Eventually, the minstrels took a break, and the

roar of conversation rose to replace the sound of music.

"I'm surprised to see you here, Rune," Valdar said, leaning back in his chair.

I arched a meaningful brow at Rune, but he ignored me. Instead, he took a long gulp of his ale, like he was stalling. He probably was.

When he finally set down his tankard, he said, "I'm here often. Guess it's been too packed for you to notice."

The skin between Rune's brow pinched, and he looked away. He was lying right through his teeth about coming here often, and the skepticism on Valdar's face only confirmed it. Rune wasn't exactly the kind of person to blend in when he went somewhere.

"Sure, all right," Valdar said, frowning. "Listen, I'm going to grab another ale. You two want a refill?"

Rune looked at me. I smiled and said, "That would be lovely, thank you."

As soon as Valdar stood and vanished into the throng, Rune leaned sideways with a glint in his brown eyes. "He seems to like you. Any interest there on your side?"

I scrunched up my nose. "Where in fate's name did you get that?"

"He offered to buy you a drink," said Rune, his voice full of meaning.

"He offered to buy us *both* a drink."

"Only because I'm sitting here. It would have been rude to ignore me. Want me to leave so you can get to know him?"

"What are you *on* about?" I shook my head, searching his expression for a sign that he was joking. And while he looked amused, he seemed to mean what he'd said. I cast my mind back to the moments before Valdar got up. The fire demon had seemed friendly enough, but it wasn't like he was *flirting*....oh.

Rune and his bloody traps. He couldn't even sit back and enjoy the minstrels, so focused was he on tightening the noose around my neck. Though...I could hardly blame him. In his shoes, I'd probably do the same thing.

"I really don't think he's interested, Rune," I said, shrugging. "Besides, he's not really my type, anyway."

"Oh? And what is your type?"

"I don't know. It's not a physical thing. I go for all types in that regard. But there's got to be that spark. Someone who stirs something in me. It's hard to put into words."

"And he doesn't give off sparks to you?" he asked.

"Not at the moment, no."

"Most of the single folk in Oakwater would beg to differ," Rune said wryly.

"Sounds like he's got enough folk going for him, then."

"Admittedly, he *is* over there, chatting up a pretty dwarf by the bar," he said in a low voice, gesturing through a break in the crowd.

They were in an animated discussion, seemingly oblivious to everyone around them. I nodded, elbowing Rune in the side. "See, that's what I'm talking about. They've got that spark." I smiled when Valdar boomed his laughter, and the dwarven girl giggled with her hand on her mouth. "Good for them."

"Except I don't think we're getting that round of ales now," Rune said.

My smile widened. "No, I don't think we are."

A beat passed. "Are you really a fan of Silva Sweetwater?"

"Honestly? The biggest. I own almost her entire catalog, including some rare editions that are no longer in print. There's only one title I don't have. *The Orc's Bride.* I've spent years trying to find it, but so many of that one got destroyed back during Isveig's war..." My voice cracked, and I fell silent, tears stinging my eyes. It suddenly hit me that I was speaking as if those books were still mine. Like

I could flip open their pages and read Silva's words anytime I wanted—anytime I *needed* them. Because while I'd lived my life alone in my cottage, I'd always had her characters. I'd come to love them as though they were my own friends.

"Well, I suppose I don't have any of them now," I said quietly.

Rune frowned. "Sounds like they mean a lot to you."

"I know it must seem silly to you, but those books were there for me when no one else was. They're about love and friendship and finding your way in the world when everything seems stacked against you. I used to reread a couple of them once a year. In the summer, I'd grab a blanket and a book and go down to the lake. But I guess I won't be doing that any longer…"

No, once I became an official member of the guild, I'd never read another word of a Silva Sweetwater novel. Or any other novel, for that matter. And while I'd *known* this—while I'd even taken the vows—it hadn't really hit me until now.

Rune grunted, then stood.

I frowned up at him, and he towered over me with his husks glinting in the dim lighting. "Where are you going?"

"I'm going to get you that ale." With a firm nod, he moved away from the table. I watched him push through the crowd. Despite his bulk, he didn't shove others out of the way like a lesser man might. Instead, he gently wended through the throng disturbing no one else at all. Valdar saw him approach, pounded him on the back, then passed him two tankards.

By the time Rune returned to the tables, the minstrels had started their second set. We clinked our tankards together. I nearly downed the entire thing in one gulp, feeling the urge to drown my sorrows. I expected Rune to question me some more, to ask why I'd left a life and a home I so clearly loved. But he seemed to sense my melancholy and took to enjoying the show instead.

And so we sat there together, drinking ale and listening to the lilting pixie's voice as she sang about the dwarves who lived under the mountain, their yearly contest to find the fittest among them, and their glowing gemstones that powered their underground world. Rune and I listened with rapt attention, occasionally exchanging a few words. When I found myself smiling after he told me another unexpected joke, I realized I was enjoying his company far more than I ought.

Maybe that would be all right, just for one night.

IO

FRIDA

"Thank you for a lovely night," I said, almost prancing along the road that led back to Rune's cottage. I wondered if I might be slurring my words a bit, then found I didn't really mind if I was. A warm sense of contentment seemed to swirl through me. I didn't know if it was from the ale, the music, or the many lovely people I'd met this night. Perhaps it was all of it combined.

"Glad you enjoyed it," he said gruffly.

I cast him a sideways glance. "Did *you*?"

"Unexpectedly, yes. It's been a long time since I…spent so long out on a Freyasday evening."

"Ha. I see right through you, Rune," I said, poking him in the arm. Wow, it was hard as a rock.

Even his muscles had muscles. "You don't need to pretend you go there every week. I know you only went tonight because you wanted to take me."

He grunted but made no attempt to rebuke my claim. Anything else he'd planned to say was interrupted by the sudden crash of thunder. The wind had picked up, dusting dirt against my legs and tugging leaves off the branches of the trees. I tipped back my head to gaze up at the sky, and an impenetrable darkness stared back at me.

Rune suddenly gripped my arm. "We need to move quickly. A storm's coming."

My heart leapt at the panic in his voice. "If it starts raining, will it hurt your skin?"

"Oh yes. But that's not what I'm worried about."

A harsh wind suddenly gusted into us, and Rune tugged me into his chest. He wrapped his arms around me, as if to protect me from the onslaught of the storm. His warmth and strength consumed me, and the scent of wood shavings filled my head, making me feel a bit dumbstruck for a moment. I swallowed, my face still pressed into his chest. I should really move away...

"Come on," he said, urging me down the path. He didn't release me, and I didn't pull away.

"You're scaring me, Rune," I eventually said.

"Good. The Elding is nothing to trifle with."

"The Elding?" I asked, alarmed. "I thought that was nothing more than a folktale. A myth meant to keep people away from the Isles."

"Oh, it's no myth. It's as real as the sun on your face in the morning. And you don't want to be outside when it hits. The wind is strong enough to fell trees, even those redwoods."

"You sound like you're speaking from experience."

"I got caught out in it once, and I'll never make that mistake again. As you can imagine, it nearly killed me."

I fell silent, my heart pounding angrily in my chest. The Elding was a storm of legend. Some believed the magic of the islands had conjured it as a way to protect its inhabitants from those who meant them harm. Others believed it was a punishment from the Old Gods, toward those who had turned their backs on their ways. I'd always just thought it was a fairy tale.

Apparently not.

By the time we'd made it back to the cottage, the wind had picked up considerably. We reached Rune's front door just as the rain began to pour and another crash of thunder tore through the sky. The droplets pelted against him—and me—but despite the agony he must feel, Rune made no sound. He threw open the door and motioned me inside first.

I stumbled into the safe haven of his cottage. Rune thundered in behind me and slammed the door shut. A moment later, he lowered a heavy latch over the wood. Wind rattled the door against its hinges, and the rain roared, as fierce and deadly as a dragon.

Rune grabbed the darkened oil lamp hanging beside the door. After lighting the wick, he swept the lamp from side to side, illuminating the interior of his cottage. With a pitiful meow, his cat raced across the floor, climbed up his leg, and launched into the crook of his elbow. With another meow, she buried her face in his arm. Her little body trembled, black hair flying everywhere.

"There you are. It's all right, Moira," he said, gently scratching the feline beneath the chin.

My heart thundered as I stared at him. Red welts decorated his throat and arms, but the largest hissed angrily on his right cheek. He barely seemed to notice, too focused on worrying over his cat.

"You're hurt," I said.

Rune looked up, his brow pinched. Then his eyes drifted to his arms, like he was only just noticing the wounds. "This is nothing compared to how bad they get sometimes. Besides, I've got some healing salve for them. They'll be gone within a couple of days."

But instead of going for his salve, Rune hung

the oil lamp on the wall and went into the corner behind the dining table. He rustled around in the cupboards before extracting a bowl, adding some milk to it, and placing it on the floor for his cat.

Moira stayed where she was. When he tried to encourage her toward the bowl, she hissed at him.

"You damn cat," he murmured, affection coating every word.

"Where do you keep it?" I asked, still standing slightly useless in the middle of the cottage.

He frowned over at me. "Where do I keep what?"

"Your *salve*," I said. "For your wounds?"

"It's in my bedroom." He turned his attention back to his cat once more. "But worry about that later. You're soaking wet. Get changed into some dry clothes before you catch a cold."

I opened my mouth to argue with him. His wounds were a vicious shade of red. And while my clothes were damp, so were his. The longer he waited to change, the more likely the water would seep through his tunic and cause more welts to form.

But with the way he looked at his cat, I knew he'd do nothing until she'd calmed down.

Shaking my head, I padded into my room and quickly changed into the only other comfortable clothes I'd packed. It was an almost-identical ensemble to the one I already wore. When I returned to the main room, Moira still hadn't budged. She'd even latched her claws in his shirt. Rune spoke to her in a quiet, steady voice. As distracted as he was, he didn't notice when I crossed the room and pushed through the only other door.

The dim light from the oil lamp barely stretched this far, so I left the door open when I inched into Rune's bedroom. The scent of him pulsed against my senses, a heady mixture of wood shavings, smoke, and leather. My heart began to pound. Casting my gaze around the small room, I found a bed—much like the one in the guest room—and a side table overflowing with a teetering stack of books.

The only other piece of furniture was a chest of drawers, clearly handmade like all the other wooden structures inside this house. Dozens of carved dragon figurines perched on top. Some were painted in vibrant shades of oranges and golds, while others had been left untouched. Just beside them sat a stack of small metal tins.

I cast a quick glance out the door. From here, I couldn't see him, so I had no idea if he was coming. He could appear in the doorway at any moment. The urge to rifle through his drawers was nearly overwhelming, but I tamped down the urge.

Instead, I picked up a few of the dragon statues, turned them over in my hand, and examined every whittled curve of them. Rune *must* have a dragon. Why else would he carve statue after statue of this one particular creature? There were no other figurines in his room. No wolves or horses. No cats.

Just dragons.

That had to mean something.

Heavy footsteps thundered across the floor of the main room. I dropped the figurine, snatched the nearest tin, and bustled over to the doorway just as Rune reached it himself. He scowled down at me, then looked over my shoulder at his bedroom. His gaze immediately swung to his chest of drawers, right where the dragon figurines watched us from the shadows.

"What the fuck are you doing in my bedroom?" he growled, his lips curling around his tusks.

I held up the tin, smiling tightly. "Getting your salve for you. I'm guessing it's in here?"

He narrowed his eyes. "I don't mind you staying at my house, but you can't just barge into my room anytime you like."

"I'd hardly call it *barging*."

"Just don't go in there. All right?"

"Sure." I skirted past him, somehow managing to squeeze past his body. The cat was on the floor now, eagerly lapping up the milk Rune had set out for her. The image of Rune fussing over her came rushing back. The gentle way he'd held her, calming down her terror of the storm. It tugged at my heartstrings and made me wish I could just *ask* him about the dragon. No more traps. No more games. I so badly wanted to get everything out on the table, so we could somehow move on from here.

So, Rune, where's that dragon of yours, and do you mind if I borrow it for a little while? Don't worry. I'm not here to assassinate you. And even if I was, you're far too kind for a head-chopping!

I sighed. If only it could be as easy as that.

If only my family were a part of something like…the Cheese Guild. Then I wouldn't have to worry about stealing something, let alone facing the first time I had to shoot an arrow into someone's head. We could just sit around the dinner table, tasting all manner of cheese from around the world. And *that* guild would never enforce any vows of celibacy or demand their members give up Silva Sweetwater novels.

"Frida? Everything all right?" Rune came up behind me. I realized I'd been standing dumbly in the middle of his cottage for a moment longer than what might be considered normal.

"Yes, hi." Pasting on a bright smile, I spun

toward him. "We need to sort out your wounds. Sit."

"Let me get the fire going." He stepped around me, moving toward the hearth.

"Rune," I said. "You're *wounded*. Please let me help you."

He grunted. "Just let me start the fire, and then you can fuss over the welts all you like."

"I'm not fussing," I said. Assassins and thieves didn't fuss. And if they did, they certainly didn't do so over their marks. Sighing, I shook my head at myself. This was such a mess.

Still, I waited while he lit the fire. After a few moments, flames roared in the hearth, casting a soothing heat through the room. Rune stood and lumbered over to the chair. When he sat heavily on its frame, he looked up at me expectantly.

"Go on then," he said.

I rolled my eyes, kneeling before him. "You act like I'm being unreasonable when all I'm trying to do is help you. You must be in pain."

"When you've dealt with these things as long as I have, you get used to it." His gaze met mine, and the tension around his eyes softened. "But I do appreciate what you're doing. I normally just let them fester, which makes them stick around a long time."

"So they *do* hurt," I said, spinning the lid off the tin.

He shifted uneasily on the chair. "A bit."

I took that to mean they stung like scorpions. He just didn't want to admit it, least of all to someone he thought was here to take something from him. Fair enough. Gently, I spread my fingers across the dark green salve, and the scent of brine, mud, and crushed leaves filled the air. After I had a good glob of it, I leaned forward and gently brushed it across one of the welts on his neck.

Rune flinched, hissing between his clenched teeth.

I stilled, then sat back on my heels. "Sorry, I'm trying to be gentle."

"It only stings when you first touch it. That one's starting to feel better already." He gave me a nod. "Keep going."

I leaned back in. Up close, his skin was such a soft shade of moss, illuminated by the glow of the hearth-fire. His face was only inches from mine, and my eyes were caught for a moment on his full lips and the glint of the tusks that curved in each corner of them. The tips were deadly sharp, and if he wanted, he could easily ensnare me with one.

My pulse thrummed in my neck, and I turned my attention to the next welt. With timid fingers, I dabbed more salve onto the wound. He didn't make a noise this time, though his cheeks twitched, as if he were clenching his jaw as tightly as possible.

Carefully, I covered each welt with more of the salve until I'd tended to every one. Rune loosed a long, rattling sigh when I put the cap back on the tin. He eased into his chair and closed his eyes.

"Thank you for that," he said.

"You're welcome." I went to stand, but he grabbed my hand. His touch was gentle, yet firm.

"I mean it, Frida. You didn't have to do this. I appreciate that you did."

Heat consumed my face. "It's not that big of a deal. You would have done the same for me."

"Hmm. You tired?"

"Very," I said. "Actually, I think I'll try to get some sleep now, unless there's anything else you need."

He shook his head. "Night, Frida. Get some rest."

I started to walk away, but the rocking chair suddenly creaked, putting a halt to my steps. Rune's heavy footsteps soon sounded.

"Wait," he said. "Take this."

I turned to find Rune by his bookshelves. He searched the array of books, then pulled a leather-bound tome from the highest shelf.

"What's this?" I asked.

"It's no Silva Sweetwater, but I think you might like it." A small smile danced across his lips. "It's a romance novel."

"*You* have a romance novel?"

"I've got a couple. Granted, I didn't know what they were when I bought them." He held it out to me. "Want to have it?"

My heart swelled. A smile stretched across my lips as I dashed across the room, took the book, and held it against my chest. I hadn't read a book in well over a year, thanks to my new position in the guild. Reading one here was still against the rules, of course, but…they'd never have to know.

"Thank you, Rune," I breathed. "Genuinely, you have no idea what this means to me."

He swallowed and looked away. "Hmm. Well, you're welcome. Now go on. I'm pretty tired myself."

I took that as my cue to get out of his hair. We'd spent every moment of the day together. He was likely sick of my company by now. Fine with me. I had a novel to read. A *novel*. With romance and adventure and hopefully a bit of spice.

Grinning, I minced across the floor to my bedroom door. When I reached it, I cast another glance over my shoulder. Rune still stood by his shelves, staring after me. The hearth-light danced across his features and highlighted his broad shoulders, the powerful flex of his arms, and the endless brown of his eyes.

And if I was being honest—which I *definitely* wasn't going to be—I might admit that he looked an awful lot like a romance novel hero himself.

II

FRIDA

Despite my every intention to read the entire book in one sitting, I only got a chapter in before my heavy eyelids refused to open again. At some point, the book slid from my fingers and tumbled to the floor, but even that didn't wake me.

Several hours later, it was the glowing light of the oil lamp that finally pushed through the fog of sleep. I cracked open my eyes, squinting into its insistent yellow flame. Rain and wind still pounded against the side of the house, and the wooden walls groaned in response. I flopped onto my back and stared up at the low ceiling. Despite the storm, I felt safe and warm inside this cottage. And more at peace than I'd felt in months.

But then I thought of what I'd come here to do. It was like a bucket of ice on the small flame of hope I'd kindled.

Rune was nothing like the guild's normal marks. I knew it in my bones, even if I'd never been on an assignment until now. My brother and father had regaled me with enough stories over the past year that I knew one thing for certain: everything about this situation was *highly* irregular.

There was more to this story—far more than what Erik had told me. This wasn't about the dragon. It was about Rune, and I hadn't the foggiest clue what to do about it. The only thing I knew for certain was that things couldn't continue as they were. I couldn't stay with Rune for three weeks, pretend to be his assistant, and then turn the tables on him. It felt *wrong*.

If I stole his dragon, it would be the ultimate betrayal of his kindness.

I knew he didn't trust me, and I knew he was trying to confirm his suspicions. But he'd still treated me with decency when he truly didn't need to. The longer I stayed here, the worse I would feel when I had to take something from him—something that was clearly important to him. He wouldn't have carved all those dragon figurines if the creature didn't mean the world to him.

Which meant I couldn't waste any more time with my investigations. Unlike me, Rune was likely cocooned in a heavy slumber right now. With all that ale running through him, he'd be dead to the world. This might be my only chance to poke around his house without his supervision. I had a feeling that tomorrow he'd watch my every move like a hawk, just like he had today. Perhaps he'd left something lying around to indicate where he kept his dragon.

My bones screamed at me as I threw aside the covers and crawled out of bed. Cool air brushed my skin, bringing forth a shiver. A linen dressing gown hung on the back of the door, which I gladly threw over my shoulders. It was several sizes too big, and the soft material practically drowned my body. The bottom of it even dragged across the floor when I padded out of the room.

Embers glowed in the hearth, and the scent of wood smoke still lingered. Moira was curled up in Rune's rocking chair, basking in the fading warmth. When I eased across the floorboards, she pried open her eyes, took one look at me, and promptly went back to sleep. I released a breath and moved toward Rune's work table.

In the dim lighting, an opaque gray washed out the details of my surroundings. I squinted to study

Rune's drawings, but the shapes were meaningless without a lamp. I briefly wondered if I should fetch the oil lamp from my room, then thought better of it. Instead, I pulled one of the drawers open and felt around inside. My fingers brushed across a few tools, but there were no hidden parchments with detailed instructions on where to find a dragon.

I gently shut the drawer and looked around. My gaze shifted to the far wall with its floor-to-ceiling bookshelves. Could the answers be hidden between the pages of one of those tomes? Did Rune keep a journal, perhaps?

I'd made it halfway across the room when the timber floorboards creaked behind me. Heart lurching, I froze in place, and a shiver of panic tore down my spine.

"Want to tell me what you're doing?" Rune's voice rumbled in the heavy silence.

Swallowing, I turned to face him. In the darkness, it was impossible to read his expression. The shadows brushed across his jaw, veiling all his features—everything except the tusks that caught the light of the burning embers.

"I…" My mind grasped onto the first thing that popped into my head. "I'm hungry. I wanted a midnight snack."

A long beat passed before he answered. "You know I don't keep food at my woodworking table."

"It's dark. I got turned around."

"And that's why you're heading to the book-shelves now instead of the food cupboards," he said dryly.

"Oh, are those the shelves?" I emitted a nervous laugh. "Guess I won't find any cheese over there…"

"I put the cheese in the food cupboard. You watched me do it." With a grunt, he crossed the room to said cupboard and yanked it open. He pointed inside, where the cheese was, in fact, waiting for me. "If you want some, you're welcome to it anytime, but you won't find it rifling around in my work drawers."

Shit. He must have seen me far before I'd heard him. It was impressive that he could move that silently, as broad and muscular as he was. The only other folk I knew with that kind of stealth had trained in it. More evidence that Rune had once been a member of the Assassin's Guild. And if that were the case, Erik knew it, too.

The question rose to my tongue. I was desperate to ask. But I knew once I did, there would be no turning back. I'd have to finish the job or leave empty-handed. Neither option was particularly appealing to me right now.

Instead, I slowly walked toward the food cupboard. Rune waited beside it with his gaze pinned on my face. When I pushed up onto my toes to reach the cheese, I could still feel his eyes on me. It made my neck burn, and sweat coated my palms.

I took some cheese from the cupboard, but it slipped through my fingers and fell with a thud against the timber floorboards.

Heartbeat loud in my ears, I went to pick it up, but Rune had already beaten me to it. He knelt on one knee, plucked the cheese from the floor, and looked up at me. Something dark passed through his eyes, making my breath catch. Then he slowly stood and pressed the cheese into my hand.

Despite the warmth of his skin, I shivered when his fingers brushed mine.

"Thanks," I said softly.

"I'd be careful about dropping that again," he murmured, inclining his head toward his sleeping cat. "Moira is also a big fan of Arvid's cheese."

A smile tickled my lips. "Of course she is."

His eyes locked on mine, Rune gently took my shoulders and turned me around so that I faced the opposite direction. And if I'd thought my heart was pounding before, it was nothing compared to now. It was like a drum was echoing inside my skull.

"Do you think you can find the way to your bedroom, or do you need a chaperone?" he asked.

His hands were warm on my shoulders, and an

errant, unwanted thought tore through my mind. It had been so long since I'd touched anyone—or been touched. And when I returned to the guild, I'd rarely get the chance to venture further than a few streets away from the guild-hall. Most assignments were contained within the city walls. With all those eyes keeping tabs on me, I'd never find an opportunity to...skirt the boundaries of my vow.

My pulse pounded in my neck. What in fate's name was I thinking? I couldn't skirt the rules *now*, either. Not like that. And even if I could, it certainly wouldn't be with my mark. I must be delirious from lack of sleep. That was the only logical explanation for the direction of my thoughts.

"I think I can manage just fine on my own," I squeaked.

Rune's breath was hot on the back of my neck, sparking heat within me. After a long, excruciating moment stretched between us, he slid his hands off my shoulders. His knuckles skated along the edge of my arm, then his touch vanished. Instantly, I felt his lack of warmth like an icy wave crashing over me.

I swallowed hard and hurried across the floor, knowing I was giving myself away by how quickly I moved. But I felt so on edge. I needed to put some space between me and Rune. And a door. A very shut door. One that would stand against my lurid thoughts, too.

"Good night, Frida," Rune murmured.

Something about the way he said my name sounded like a promise.

12

RUNE

Moira weaved through my legs while I stood by a pot hanging over the hearth-fire. I stirred the eggs that sizzled inside, whistling one of the tunes we'd heard at the tavern last night. After I'd found Frida lurking around my woodworking table, sleep had eluded me, but now I felt a bit like I'd guzzled a bucket of Galdur sand. This was the most energized I'd felt in months.

I tried not to dwell on why that was, but I struggled to get the image of Frida's heart-shaped face out of my mind. Last night had been genuinely enjoyable, and I usually hated crowds. Sure, she'd poked around the cottage after I'd fallen asleep… which had increased my suspicions, but I could acknowledge it had been dark. She might have gotten turned around.

And I definitely hadn't minded when she'd practically *thrummed* beneath my touch. I couldn't be sure I hadn't imagined that part, though. In the fresh light of day, Frida's reaction almost felt like a dream.

A very good dream, I hated to admit.

"Something smells heavenly," said Frida.

My eyes were instantly drawn to her. She stood in the doorway of the guest bedroom—*her* bedroom now. Her hair was unbound and spilling over her shoulders in soft waves. She'd already changed back into her clothes. Her leathers again rather than the tunics and trousers she'd worn yesterday.

She noticed my attention had gone to the leather straps that encircled her upper thigh. Blushing, she said, "About this. I thought…perhaps I'm overstaying my welcome here."

I frowned. "What are you talking about? You're my assistant, which means you lodge here in this cottage so you can be on hand to help when I need it. And to be honest, that's basically all the damn time until that fence gets built."

"Surely you don't want me to stay here for weeks, let alone longer than that." She nibbled on her bottom lip.

"Why wouldn't I? You're my assistant. Besides, where else would you go? The inn's full."

"I thought I could just camp out in the woods," she said.

I searched her gaze. "Is this about last night?"

"What?" Her blush deepened. "No."

So then it was. Which part of it, though? The part where I'd caught her poking around or the part where I'd almost scraped my lips across the back of her neck? The part where I'd felt the want burning between us.

"I don't mind if you get up in the middle of the night for a snack," I said slowly.

She gave me a look. "You clearly thought I was sneaking around and looking in your drawers."

I arched a brow. "And were you?"

"Well, a little bit." She shifted uneasily on her feet. "I fell asleep with the lamp still on, and it woke me up. I didn't think I'd be able to fall back asleep right away, so I...decided to look around."

"I see." I turned back to the pot and pulled it off the fire. The eggs were glistening and ready to eat.

"Which means I betrayed your trust. I really oughtn't take advantage of your hospitality like this," she said quietly.

"Frida, it's fine. While I don't like you poking around my things, I've got nothing to hide. Just don't do it again."

A tense moment passed, the cottage silent other than the clinking of dishes while I served up breakfast. I'd put together a feast of eggs, bacon, and buttered potatoes, along with some of that cheese she loved so much. The kettle whistled, ready for me to brew the tea.

"I thought you'd be angry and want me to leave." Her eyes tracked my every move, but she hadn't budged from her bedroom door.

"Well, I'm not." I sank into the nearest chair and motioned at the array of food I'd laid out on the table. "So, are you going to join me, or are you going to make me eat all this by myself?"

She pressed her lips together, then said. "You do sound a bit annoyed."

"I'll be more annoyed if you insist on camping out in the forest alone, especially with the Elding coming last night. It'll probably storm a few more nights before it fully moves on to somewhere else. And then I'd worry about your safety, so I'd search the forest until I found you." I pointed at my arm, where the welts were already beginning to fade. "Then I'd get a lot more of these things. Just do me a favor and stay."

"Very manipulative," she said. But then she crossed the room, took the chair across from mine, and reached for the cheese. "You know, you could just be honest and tell me you need me to stay so that I can sketch the house build for you."

I nearly choked on my sudden burst of laughter. "That would be an arrestable offense. No matter that we haven't arrested anyone in Oakwater in well over a decade. We'd open up the jail just for you."

"Well, I do need somewhere to live."

"Maybe I should just chain you up in my cellar instead." I quirked a smile.

"Sounds awfully tempting. Is there any cheese down there?"

"No. And if you try to draw a house, I'll eat all the damn cheese myself."

With a delighted laugh, Frida grabbed the cheese wheel and clutched it against her chest. Then her eyes went as wild and wide as the moon, and she stuffed the whole thing down the front of her shirt.

"There." She leaned across the table, her eyes dancing. "You want it? Come and get it."

"Hmm. What was it you said? Sounds awfully tempting. Especially because I know there *is* cheese down there."

Her face broke out into a smile so wide that I decided something right then and there. Frida couldn't be a killer. There was a light inside her, and it shone through her eyes. Assassins lost that the first time they watched the light die in someone else's, especially when it was by their own hands.

My gut told me she had secrets. Something about her story didn't quite add up, and I found it hard to believe her striking resemblance to the Rurik family was merely a coincidence. I didn't know the full truth about her yet, but I was certain she was no killer.

While I'd sat there contemplating her, Frida'd already dug into her food. Her appetite was adorably ravenous. A mountain of eggs, bacon, and potatoes towered on her plate. A few bits of egg peppered the ground, upon which Moira happily pounced. The damn cat acted like I didn't feed her half the time.

"Here, want some more?" Frida asked sweetly, passing a glob of eggs to my cat. I shook my head, though a smile tickled the corners of my lips.

"She seems to like you," I said.

"Good. I like her, too. Really, I like most animals."

"Only most?"

"Well, I'm not sure how I'd feel about meeting a dragon." She gave me a funny look, pausing with her fork halfway to her mouth. "What about you? Do you like dragons?"

What an odd question.

"Suppose I've got no reason to dislike them," I said.

A thundering sounded on the door, putting a momentary pause on our conversation. I rose from the table and went to answer it. And as the pounding grew louder, I frowned. I normally didn't get visitors, especially this time in the morning, and especially not with knocking that was so frantic.

When I yanked open the door, I found Valdar on the front stoop, his paled face glistening with sweat. Beyond him, felled branches littered my garden and a chunk of my workshop lay in ruins. My stomach twisted painfully.

"Sorry to bother you, Rune. I can see you've got your own damage to deal with, but we need your help," Valdar said, his voice thin.

I dragged my attention away from my garden, my gaze landing on Valdar's eyes. They were so wide, the whites nearly consumed them. "Help with what?"

"The Elding's winds were bad last night, Rune." Valdar ran a hand along the length of his red horns, grimacing. "Helga's house has collapsed. With her in it."

13

FRIDA

"I've got to go." Rune thundered over to his woodworking table and hauled an axe from the row of tools lined up along the wall.

I slowly stood. Moira weaved between my legs, clearly hoping I'd drop some more egg. "Why? What's going on?"

"Someone's trapped inside a fallen building in town. I've got to get them out."

My heart lurched into my throat. "I'm coming with you."

With a snarl, he paused halfway to the open door, where I spotted Valdar waiting and wringing his hands. I braced myself for Rune's rebuke. His body practically hummed with rage, like he was seconds away from ripping off the head of the next person who annoyed him. And unfortunately, that was probably me.

"Grab that rope, a waterskin, and a towel." He jerked his thumb over his shoulder at his work-table. "And get your bow, just in case. Don't fall behind."

Without another word, Rune stormed outside. I swallowed the lump in my throat, then scurried through the cottage to collect the items he'd listed. By the time I made it through the door, Rune and Valdar were already vanishing through the trees. With my quiver bouncing on my back, I dashed after them.

On my way, I had to leap over shredded branches that were scattered around Rune's garden and weave past his workshop. A larger branch had fallen against one wall, smashing a few beams. The sight of it forced my feet to slow. It would take hours to salvage—if he could even salvage it. My heart hurt for him. I'd seen the glint of pride in his eyes when he spoke about this place. He'd put so much time and effort into it, and he'd clearly crafted it with loving hands to build the home of his dreams.

I shook my head and started off again. When I caught up with Rune and Valdar, they were entombed in a stony silence. Questions tumbled around my mind, but I kept them contained.

Neither of them looked like they'd welcome a volley of questions right now.

When we reached the village square, the collapsed house marred the line of buildings like a plume of smoke against a clear blue sky. A crowd hovered around it. Two elven women were sobbing, their arms flung around each other. A few other folk stalked around the perimeter and pointed at a tiny opening between the fallen planks of wood. When one of them looked our way and spotted Rune, they waved us over.

Rune led the way, marching with fierce determination.

"Glad you're here, Rune," the shadow demon said, his dark eyes sweeping across our group. "Helga's trapped inside. We can't get to her without putting her at risk of getting crushed."

Rune grunted, then shoved past the demon. He was the minstrel I'd noticed on stage last night, though that familiar spark I swore I'd felt when I saw him was gone now. Nothing about him seemed familiar. Unlike most shadow demons I'd met, he'd shorn his hair to his scalp, which had the effect of making his curving horns look twice as large. It might have come across as intimidating if it weren't for the tunic he wore. It was made entirely from wildflowers.

"Frida, I need your help," Rune called over his shoulder.

He squatted beside the fallen house with his arms shoved into the gap. It was then I noticed how wet everything was. Rain had soaked the world, and condensation still clung to the patches of grass surrounding the house—right where Rune's knees dug into the ground. Rivulets of rainwater curled down the broken planks of wood and pooled on his arms. The water hissed where it made contact, but Rune didn't so much as flinch.

I hurried over to him, my heart leaping in my chest. "Can you reach her?"

"No. She's too far back."

"Then get your arms out of there," I scolded him.

He grimaced, then gave me an almost imperceptible head tilt, like he was motioning for me to come closer. I leaned forward and tried to ignore the heat emanating from his body, a heat that urged me to draw even closer.

"I might be a bit stuck," he murmured.

My eyes widened. "You can't be serious."

"Unfortunately, I'm as serious about this as you are about cheese." A ghost of a smile flickered across his lips. "Think you could help me out?"

I knelt beside him and wrapped my hands around his biceps. A sudden tremor went through me. His face was only inches from mine—so close I could see flecks of gold in his brown eyes and catch the lingering scent of smoke from this morning's hearth-fire. Despite the weight of the entire village's gaze on us, it suddenly felt like we were alone, and the roaring of my heart drowned out the whispers and shuffling of feet.

And then I blinked, and everything came rushing back in around us.

I swallowed. "Right. I'm going to pull really hard. I need you to brace yourself. Are you ready?"

Rune nodded.

"On the count of three." I tightened my grip on his arm. "Three. Two. One—"

With a very unladylike groan, I put every ounce of strength into yanking at his arm. For a moment, I thought nothing would happen, that his arm would never budge. But then something gave way, and his arm scraped free of the broken wood. Blood bubbled from the line of scratches along his arm, but it was nothing compared to the dozen welts scattered amongst them. I hissed between clenched teeth, but Rune barely seemed to notice the pain. He shifted sideways, angling his body just so, and pulled the other arm out of the gap. Angry red consumed that arm, too.

The sound of muffled sobs drifted toward us, and tension tightened Rune's face.

"Helga, it's all right," he called out. "Don't you worry. We're going to get you out of there."

Her sobs quietened.

Ignoring the wounds, Rune grabbed the edge of the beam and shook it, testing the weight of it. "I need you and Valdar to hold this piece up while I try going inside again."

I squinted at him. "That's a completely nonsensical idea. Let me go instead. I think I can actually fit through without tossing beams around and making the whole thing collapse."

"You want to go in there instead?" He jerked his head my way, looking genuinely surprised. I tried not to take it as an insult.

"*Yes*. I sometimes explored the forest caves back home, and this gap is perfectly suitable for someone my size."

He got that look on his face again. The one that was nearly impossible to read but told me a flurry of thoughts was going through his mind. Eventually, he shook his head and stood.

"All right, but I'm going to hold up this plank, just in case," he said.

I thought about telling him to tend to his wounds instead, but I knew he'd ignore that as surely as I'd ignore an attempt to talk me out of crawling inside the building. Besides, now was not the time to get into a bickering match with my mark. A rustling sounded from within the house. Helga was clearly panicked and attempting to escape her confinement. If someone didn't get to her soon, I worried she'd cause the building to collapse even further.

I shrugged off my quiver and piled it on top of the blanket, nodding at Rune to let him know I was ready. Clenching his jaw, he strained against the plank of wood, and the gap into the house slightly widened.

I crawled forward into the shadows. Something sharp pierced my trousers, and a painful scrape went through my left knee. Gritting my teeth, I continued forward, mud smearing across my palms. A beam knocked my head, and I winced. Through the haze, I spotted the flaming red hair of the dwarven woman I'd seen flirting with Valdar last night. She squirmed where she'd been trapped by a ceiling beam.

"Hey there," I said, inching toward her. She'd gotten pinned into place on her side, her elbow and cheek smashed against the ground. Up close, I could see it was only her foot stuck beneath the beam, though there was a bright, hot pain flickering in her eyes.

She sucked a sharp breath in through her nose, peering up at me. "You're Rune's new assistant."

"That's right. And I'm going to get you out of here. I just need you to tell me what hurts."

"My foot. I think it's broken."

I nodded and crawled closer to her foot, ignoring another flash of pain in my knee. The sturdy leather boot hit her mid-calf, but it was wide at the top. "I'm going to do something, and you're probably going to hate me for it."

"Let me guess," she said dryly. "You want me to pull my foot out of my boot."

"I'll be the one to pull it out of there, but yes. It's the best way to free you without risking the stability of the house."

Helga's laugh was low, rough. "Pretty sure the Elding already took care of the stability of this house."

"Will you let me do it?" I asked.

She closed her eyes. "I don't suppose I have another option."

"What's your drink of choice?"

"Oh, I love a good sparkling wine from the Kingdom of Edda, especially this time of year when the sun invites the world to lounge beneath its warmth. On a blanket. With a book. Or a good man. Ideally, both, but you can't be too picky around here. Valdar's nice, though." She sighed.

"If you let me free your foot, I'll make sure you get all those things," I told her.

"Deal," she said without hesitating.

"Everything all right in there?" Rune gruffly called from outside.

I raised my voice so he could hear me. "Yes, we're just sorting out a plan."

"The plan is to get her out of there as soon as possible. I won't be able to hold up this plank for much longer."

Helga snorted, rolling her eyes. "I hope he's not the man you plan to put on my reading blanket. Because I don't think that'd be too relaxing, truth be told."

An unexpected emotion swelled in my chest— an odd combination of protectiveness and…well, it wasn't *jealousy*. Because that would be ridiculous. Who was I to care if Rune courted someone while I was here? It had nothing to do with me. He was my mark, and I had to steal a dragon from him.

But I still felt a flicker of *something*, and it was uncomfortable, like a splinter stuck in my toe.

"He's definitely not who I had in mind," I assured her.

"Then the deal's still on," she said. "Let's get this over with."

I wound my hands around her leg, trying my best to steady my racing heart. "Here we go."

~

When Helga and I crawled out of the broken building with mud crusting our clothes, exuberant applause drummed the air, like the beat of an upbeat tavern song. The crowd rushed forward, surrounding Helga and fussing over her broken foot. Soon, they carried her away and lifted her into the air like a queen. Valdar trotted after the procession with relief shining in his eyes.

Rune's attention, however, stayed on me. He looked me over, examining a few scrapes along my arms. When he noticed blood on my trouser knee, his brow furrowed and he scooped me up into his arms.

"That's hardly necessary," I said with a laugh.

Ignoring my protests, he motioned at Arvid, who hovered a few feet away. "You mind grabbing Frida's things and bringing them back to my cottage?"

"My pleasure," said Arvid.

Rune took off after Arvid's confirmation. His purposeful strides were long and quick, making me realize he'd been slowing his pace significantly whenever I'd walked with him. We were halfway back to the cottage before I seized control of my thoughts. It was difficult to think straight with his powerful arms wrapped possessively around my body and the scent of him filling my head. Where our skin made contact, it felt like a thousand tiny butterflies were fluttering against me. It made little sense.

Maybe I was just delirious from crawling into a fallen building.

I cleared my throat, trying to focus on anything other than the thrumming of his heartbeat in his neck. "You can put me down, Rune. I'm sure I can walk the rest of the way to your cottage."

"Your knee is bleeding," he said gruffly.

"All right, but it barely hurts. I'm sure it's just a little scratch."

"Let me take care of you, Frida. The way you took care of me when I was wounded."

"Says the orc who is currently sporting twice as many welts as he had last night."

He grunted and tightened his arms around me. "I'm carrying you home and seeing to your wounds, then we'll worry about me."

Guilt spread through me, like a particularly nasty plague. I clenched my jaw and looked away. I had no right to accept help from Rune, knowing what I'd come here to do. Sure, it was only thieving, which was nothing compared to what Erik could have ordered, but the thought of doing anything that might cause him grief churned in my gut like a pint of poison.

Poison that had been in my veins from the first moment I'd breathed the air of this world. I'd tried to escape it, but a snake couldn't shed its fangs any more than a born assassin could.

Rune's cottage appeared through the trees, and as he carried me over the fallen branches, a wild thought came to me. It was like the sprouting of a seed I hadn't realized I'd buried until now. But deep down I knew it had been there since the moment I'd met Rune and he'd shown kindness to me.

Maybe I just wouldn't do it.

I could leave without taking his dragon.

As soon as the thought poked up, I shoved it down. I couldn't even consider it as an option. Because it wasn't one. Erik and my father had made their orders clear. If I failed this assignment, I'd never join the guild, which meant I'd never see my family again.

And so I did the only thing I could: I buried the thought beneath ten feet of dirt.

I4

FRIDA

Rune lowered me into his rocking chair, then vanished into my room. When he returned, he handed me the book he'd given me the night before and moved away again, this time to stir the embers of his smouldering hearth-fire. As he stoked the flames back to life, my knee throbbed with pain. I hissed through clenched teeth and opened the book to use the written word as a distraction, the way I always had through so many rough times in my life.

"Clutch that book any harder, and you might end up ripping the spine in half," Rune grunted as he returned to my side and knelt before me.

"Sorry." I tried to relax my grip, but the throbbing pain was building into a blazing heat.

"No need to apologize. It's your book now, not

mine. Now I'm going to cut a hole in your trouser leg so we can get a look at what's going on with your knee," he said, his voice softening into a tone I'd yet to hear from him.

Swallowing, I nodded and relinquished my grip on the book, placing it on the table beside the chair.

Rune gazed up at me. Several strands of his midnight hair had sprung free from its knot, scattering into his eyes. Something fluttered in my chest.

"You're not going to read?" he asked, his voice still so gentle that I could scarcely believe it was his.

"I don't think I can concentrate on the words right now."

"All right." He nodded and went back to studying my trousers. "Do you remember the first book you read? 'Cause I keep picturing you sneaking into your parents' library and stealing a Silva Sweetwater novel off the shelves without them knowing."

I winced and looked away. "They weren't big on books. Or music. Or art of any kind. They taught me to read and write, of course, but not for pleasure. I don't think I consumed an actual novel until I was fifteen and living on my own."

"In the forest? How'd you come across them there?" With careful fingers, Rune pried the material away from my skin. A hiss of pain went through me. I focused on his words, forcing myself to remain still.

"I didn't have many close neighbors. In fact, I didn't have any at all. But there were a few cottages a mile or so away, and I stumbled upon them one day when I was out exploring. The woman there, her name is Maella, welcomed me inside for tea and biscuits. And when she realized I didn't have anyone or much of anything of my own, she sent me off with a bundle of food, blankets, and books. For the next few years, she found me every few months, bringing me more supplies until she was certain I could take care of myself."

Rune frowned. "And you were only fifteen? She should have invited you to live with her instead of sending you off into the forest all by yourself."

I smiled. "Well, she tried, but I turned her down. At the time, I was pretty stubborn about wanting to live alone."

The hiss of a blade through linen filled the air as Rune got to work on my trousers. "You talk like that's changed, but you've been pretty stubborn about wanting to live alone now, too. All that nonsense about you camping out in the forest until the inn has a free room."

I leaned back in the chair, my attention caught on the focused determination etched into every line of his face. He looked so steady and sure, like he'd done this a hundred times before, and I was struck by the certainty that this was how he looked when he worked on his builds, too. Focused, determined, confident in his work. I wasn't sure I'd ever felt that way about anything other than archery. I certainly knew I didn't feel that way about assassination. My brother had told me that would change, and I'd learn to love it the way he did. But I was beginning to wonder if he was wrong about me. Because all I'd done since arriving on this island was try to find reasons to end my assignment early.

Shaking my head, I turned my attention back to our conversation.

"My idea to camp in the woods is less about wanting to live alone," I said softly, "and more about not wanting to be a burden to you—or to anyone. But no, I don't want that solitary life anymore. Back home, I got lonely after a while. There was no one to talk to, except for the animals."

"Hmm," he said. "Is that why you came here? You wanted someone to talk to?"

"In a way."

Because beneath it all, that *was* what had brought me here. All those long years by myself had driven me to such an intense loneliness that I became willing to do whatever it took to escape from it. And so I was here, sitting before a mark who was on his hands and knees trying to patch me up.

Tears welled. Gritting my teeth, I blinked them away. But Rune caught the gloss in my eyes before I got rid of it.

"Hey," he said softly, resting his warm hand on my thigh. A sudden heat tore through me, making my breath catch. "If you're lonely, you've come to the right place. This village is full of the best folk I've ever known, and they'll soon make you feel like you're a part of this place, too. Like you've always been here. And if you want to talk? Well, let me tell you, they really know how to talk." A smile curled his lips. "So be careful what you wish for."

My breath caught. "Rune, I..." A wild, reckless need to tell him why I was here buzzed in my head, like millions of angry bees. And that was how I found myself blurting, "Do you have a dragon?"

A strange look crossed his face. And like always, I couldn't read it. "That's a very odd thing to ask someone."

"Sorry." A fiery heat filled my cheeks. "It's just, I saw all those figurines in your bedroom, and you seem awfully fond of hearth-fires, even when it's nearly summer...Plus, your neighbor's cows went missing. And I thought maybe..."

At the dark look in his eye, I fell silent. He

ignored my questions and returned his attention to my knee. Tension pulsed between us. All I could do was watch while he gently cleaned my wound and applied a healing salve. When he was done, he wrapped my leg in strips of cloth and sat back on his heels.

Whatever warmth I'd felt between us was gone now.

"Keep it dry until tomorrow. The cut is fairly shallow, so it should heal just fine," he said flatly.

I pressed my lips together, then said, "I'm sorry for asking about the dragon. If I'd known how much it would bother you, I would have kept the question to myself."

He looked away, his shoulders tensing. "The truth is, you're not far off. I did have a dragon once. Years ago, before the war. But she came to the same end as all the others. It's not something I like to think about, least of all discuss. You say you were lonely. After I lost her, so was I. And I suppose I still am."

A knock sounded on the door. Rune flinched, a muscle feathering in his jaw. "That will be Arvid with your things."

He rose and moved with jerky motions toward the door, like the weight of his painful past made his limbs too heavy to control. I gripped the edge of the rocking chair, hating that

I'd been the cause of this after everything he'd done to help me.

And much to my dismay, I could already hear Erik's voice in the back of my mind. He'd claim Rune was lying, that he still had his dragon hidden somewhere nearby. That this was just a false story to throw me off the trail.

But I'd seen Rune's face. There was no faking that kind of pain.

Rune wasn't keeping a secret dragon on this island, and that knowledge gave me a relief so palpable that I nearly doubled over. I'd found the answer, even if it wasn't the one the guild wanted. My duty here was done, and I'd solved it without needing to steal or kill. But would Erik listen? Or would he take his disappointment out on me?

Fortunately, it would be a while before the ship came back to collect me. I had nearly three weeks to untangle the web of uncertainty in my mind and figure out a way to explain this to Erik in a way he'd accept. It wasn't my fault that he'd given me an assignment *no one* could have completed. Not even he would have succeeded here. If there was no dragon, there was no dragon. I couldn't just conjure one from thin air.

The more I thought about it, the better I felt. Now I could just relax. I could help Rune with his work. And when I left, I didn't have to leave a path of destruction in my wake. I wouldn't have to *take* anything from anyone. Instead, I could give my time and actually help folk for once. But the best part? I wouldn't have to make Rune hate me.

~

The next day, Rune got straight to work on a plan to rebuild Helga's home in town. It meant pausing the construction of the newest Oakwater cottage, a home for a pair who had been waiting a while. They were a couple who owned something called the Travelling Tavern. After thirty years of near constant travel, they wanted to build a base on the Floating Forest, a home they could return to between their jaunts around the islands. When Rune brought them round for dinner, he told them it might take a couple more months to finish because of Helga's house, but they were exceedingly understanding.

"Of course, take your time!" The bright-eyed elf named Lilia practically glowed from within. She sat on the opposite side of Rune's dining table, right next to her partner, Ragnar, an elf with long crimson hair.

"Are you sure?" Rune asked. "You've been waiting a long time."

Lilia nodded emphatically. "The cottage you're

building for us isn't our permanent home, not in the same way Helga's is. We still plan to travel the Isles, especially so we can make it to Riverwold's Yule celebration most winters. So there's no rush. We just want somewhere cozy and familiar when we need to slow down now and then."

"Plus, it gives us a home base for brewing our ale," Ragnar added with a fond look at his partner.

Rune smiled, then turned to me. "Wait until you try her ale. It's some of the best."

"Well, I'm glad you like it. Since that's how we're paying you," Lilia said with a laugh.

I arched my brow at Rune. "Seems I'm not the only one willing to accept food as currency."

"When you try Lilia's ale, you'll understand. The whole village has been trying to tempt her to stick around here for years."

Ragnar cocked a grin. "Didn't someone even try to come up with a new festival just to get her to stay?"

"Oh, I forgot about that! The Dragon Festival, to be held the first day of every Skerpla." Lilia cocked her head. "That would be next month, but no one's said anything about it."

Rune shook his head. "It never got off the ground. No one took the lead in organizing it so the idea just kind of fizzled out."

"The Dragon Festival?" I asked.

"Yes, because I ah..." Lilia quickly exchanged a glance with Ragnar. "Well, I have a dragon. You likely haven't seen him around yet because he comes and goes a lot. Unlike..." She trailed off, looking uncertain.

"You have a dragon?" I repeated numbly.

Even though I'd come here specifically for a dragon, and even though I'd swallowed my doubts about their existence, Lilia's words were a shock that felt like a fist to my gut. I turned to Rune, expecting him to be as taken aback as I was, but he silently stirred his stew. Because of course he already knew. None of this was a surprise to him.

"I forgot he hung around sometimes," Rune said. "That might explain how something was pinging my wards."

"Does everyone in Oakwater know about this dragon?" I asked.

Lilia shrugged. "Of course. Why else would they call it the Dragon Festival?"

So it was common knowledge. Could *this* be why Erik was misinformed? He'd heard a dragon was on the Isles, and somehow he'd come to the conclusion that it belonged to Rune. Maybe he'd just gotten the name of its keeper wrong. Maybe Lilia's dragon was the one Erik wanted me to steal.

My leg jiggled beneath the table. I'd *just* come to terms with my failure to complete this assignment, and now a solution had fallen into my lap. I didn't have to steal from Rune. I could take Lilia's dragon instead. But as I looked into her smiling face, the thought made me sick.

Fate, I wasn't cut out for this.

"Excuse me." I shoved back my chair and scrambled to my feet. "I need some air."

"Frida, come on. Wait—" Rune started to say. But I was already across the room, yanking open the door.

"It's all right. Let her go," Lilia said softly. "Folk from the mainland are always like this when they find out dragons are alive. It scares them."

I shook my head and closed the door behind me, blocking out their words and breathing in the rich scent of the forest. This wasn't about fear, at least not of the dragons themselves. For a beautiful brief moment in time, I'd thought I had an out. My fingers had closed around a bud of hope, but it had been snatched away from me before it bloomed.

Before it even had a *hope* of blooming.

15

FRIDA

With a sigh, I crossed the garden and sat heavily on a mossy stone. The buzz of insects serenaded me. I pulled my legs up to my chest, leaning my chin on my right knee. The scent of petrichor mingled with the smoke that drifted from Rune's cottage. Insects darted through the humid air, and the rustle of the wind through leaves swallowed up the static in my head. Closing my eyes, I tried to settle my thundering heart.

When I'd trained for the guild, I'd never faced anything like this. The drills were routine affairs with clear decisions and a kind of cold formality. Emotions and moral quandaries were not a part of the deal.

An owl hooted, so loud it sounded as if it was

right beside my head. My heart leapt into my throat. Pressing a shaking hand to my chest, I loosed a nervous chuckle and looked around, and nearly startled again when I spotted the brown barn owl perched beside me on the stone.

A very familiar barn owl, the only one I'd ever seen with a patch of white on his back in the shape of a heart—or at least that was what I saw when I looked at him.

I smiled and stretched out my hand. "Ottar? What are you doing here?"

He was a very long way from home.

Ottar tip-tapped his little talons against the stone, coming closer. And that was when I noticed the folded piece of parchment attached to his left leg. Dread curled through me.

"Fuck," I muttered.

The guild kept an owlery, specifically to send messages to assassins and thieves who were out in the field. Sometimes, assignments changed or new information came to light. Could Erik have discovered the same thing I had? Did he know he'd given me the wrong mark?

Would this letter command me to steal from Lilia instead?

With a trembling hand, I unhooked the message from Ottar's leg and rolled it open.

Assassin's Guild Assignment for Frida Rurik

Disregard all previous orders. The Isles are protected by magic. It prevents anyone from travelling there who intends to harm a resident. We gave you a false reason for your journey in order to gain you access. The dragon does not exist, and you are not required to steal one. Instead, your true assignment is to assassinate Rune in accordance with guild rules.

Sucking in a sharp breath, I crumpled the parchment in my fist. Blood roared in my ears, and the world around me seemed to tilt. Erik hadn't sent me here to steal a dragon. That was why I'd found no evidence of Rune having one. It was never about that.

This was meant to be my first assassination.

My heart lurched, tears stinging my eyes. I should have known. I *had* known. Deep down, I'd suspected something was off from the moment he'd given me this damn assignment. And if I'd actually asked more questions on the ship ride over, I would have realized what I was truly up against. I would have learned of the island's magic.

"Frida?" Rune's deep voice sounded from behind me, putting pressure against the splintered glass that was my heart.

How could I turn around and look at him, knowing the true reason I was here?

"Frida?" he repeated. "Are you all right?"

"No," I choked out. I was not all right, and I didn't know if I ever would be.

My first mark—the very first life I took—was to be one of the kindest people I'd ever met. He took care of people. He built them homes without demanding trunks of gold in return. When someone was in trouble, he put himself in harm's way to help them. Perhaps he'd run from something in his past, something he wished he could undo, but he was *good* now. I knew that in my bones.

He came around to kneel in front of me, and his eyes searched mine. "What's going on?"

My fist tightened around the message. "I…" I swallowed the lump in my throat. Once I said this, there was no taking it back. All my plans…all my hopes for a future surrounded by my loved ones. They'd be gone. But as I sat on that stone, gazing into the soft eyes of my mark, I realized I never would have done it. As much as I wanted to be part of a family again, I couldn't kill for it.

"There's something I need to tell you," I whispered.

Rune nodded. "All right. Let's hear it."

"I know you already suspect me of…something. And you were right to feel that way." I sucked in a deep, steadying breath, then loosed my confession as quickly as I could. "I was sent here by a guild back home. This was to be my first assignment. An induction of sorts. They wanted me to find you and steal your dragon."

His brow furrowed. "But I—"

"Don't have a dragon. I know." I held up my fisted hand. It was shaking violently. "I just received a message. This was never about a dragon. It wasn't even about theft."

Grim understanding shuddered across Rune's face. He rose and took a step back—away from me. Away from the monster I was. "Let me guess. You're from the Assassin's Guild, and you found a way around the magic that protects the island inhabitants from harm."

"No." Heart pounding, I shoved off the stone. "I mean, yes, but no. I'm from the guild, but I didn't find a way around the magic. Erik did."

He glanced away, a muscle feathering in his jaw. "I wanted so badly to believe you weren't what I thought you were. You don't seem like the type, but here you are. Well, good job, Frida. Because despite all the evidence that was right in my face, you tricked me. I'm sure you'll do well in the guild."

"Rune," I said with a shuddering breath. He kept his gaze locked on the forest, refusing to look at me. I could hardly blame him, though. "I'm not going to do it."

For an aching moment, a tense silence thrummed between us. And then he slowly turned his gaze back my way. His expression was inscrutable. "What do you mean?"

"I mean exactly what I said. I'm not going to do it." I held up my fisted hand, then tossed the crumpled message away from me. "My entire family is a part of the guild. Fate, they've been a part of it for several centuries. If you know anything about the guild—and I believe you do—you know they don't let their members associate with anyone who isn't one. For a long time, I refused to join, but…I got so lonely, Rune. I missed my family, and I wanted to be a part of something again."

He arched a brow. "By killing."

I flinched and looked away. "It wasn't supposed to be like this. They told me their marks were always folk who had committed terrible crimes, folk who'd escaped justice. My brother believes what he's doing is actually helping the world."

"And if I'm on their list, *I* must have done something terrible," he said flatly.

"No, that's not what I'm saying. I'm trying to—"

"I have done terrible things."

My breath whistled out of me. "What?"

"A long time ago, I was a member of the guild, but I was just a thief," he said, running his hand along the top of his head. "I hated it, and eventually I decided to get out. The leader agreed. On one condition. I had to complete one final assignment. Only this one wasn't for the thieves." His gaze went hard. "It was for the assassins. So I did what they asked, and when I tried to leave, they told me my skills were far too valuable for them to lose. They said if I tried to escape, they'd stop me. And so I said *fuck that* and left anyway."

"What?" I whispered.

My mind reeled, and my thunderous heartbeat roared in my ears. This kind of trick sounded *exactly* like the kind of thing Erik would do if one of his assassins wanted to escape from the web in which he'd trapped them.

I'd never heard of an orc named Rune before Erik had given me my assignment. The guilds normally had around a dozen members each at any one time. Everyone knew everyone else's business—the good, the bad, and the excruciatingly ugly. Everyone lived on guild property, all bunched on top of each other. Few left. Those who did were reviled, and their names were repeated like swears every time something went wrong.

The wind swept through the garden, spraying

leaves across the dirt and interrupting the strained silence.

"I've never heard of you before," I said. "How is that?"

"When I left, Erik wasn't in charge yet. His father was. He tasked Erik with finding a way to convince me to stay. When he failed, he didn't want his father to know what had happened. So he told him I'd died." Rune shrugged. "That's what my contacts back in the city told me, at least. We've exchanged a few messages over the years."

"That must be why my father didn't recognize your name," I murmured. "And why Erik sent *me*, someone who had never met you. He still doesn't want anyone to know."

"He wants to get rid of me quietly."

"And that's it? That's the whole story?" I asked.

"That's the whole story, Frida."

For a long moment, the tension between us crackled like hearth-fire, but Rune's steady gaze never wavered. Either he was remarkably good at lying, or he was sincere. If I were a betting kind of girl, I'd choose the latter. At this point, there was no reason for him to hide his truth from me. He knew why I was here.

Loosing a long, ragged breath, I folded my arms and tried to think. My emotions were a wild storm inside me. Erik had sent me here on a personal vendetta that had nothing to do with the guild's official codes. Rune wasn't a criminal who had escaped the noose of the law. He was someone who'd been trapped in a world he didn't want to be a part of, one they'd tried to force on him. Someone who'd come here to build a better life for himself that didn't involve theft and killing.

And against all odds, he'd succeeded. Until now, when Erik had finally found a way to get to him.

Well, I wouldn't be the conductor to this discordant orchestra. I would return to Vilmar and tell the guild everything I'd learned here. It might just be enough to unseat Erik as the current leader, and my father could take his place.

I started back toward the cottage. Rune hastened across the ground, falling into step beside me. He took my arm and pulled me back, but there was still something gentle in his touch.

"I can't let you go back inside, Frida. Lilia and Ragnar have nothing to do with this, and I don't want to get them involved," he said quietly. "They've worked hard for their quiet life."

A spike of pain went through my heart. He thought I was wicked enough to drag two innocent brewmasters into this. "I'm just getting my things, and then I'll be gone. I won't even say goodbye to them."

His grip on my arm loosened. "You really did mean what you said, didn't you? You're not going to attempt your assignment."

"It's about ten days until the ship returns to collect me. I'll camp on the beach until then. When I return to the guild, I'll tell them you're not here."

I pulled away from him and went inside the cottage. Ragnar and Lilia huddled together at the table, exchanging feverish whispers. When they heard my footsteps, they fell silent and looked my way, but I didn't dare interact with them. Tears pooled in the corners of my eyes. If I thought too hard about what I was doing, they'd fall.

After I'd collected my pack and my arrows, I pushed outside again. Rune waited by the door with his arms folded over his broad chest. My steps slowed, and I opened my mouth to offer an apology, but stopped when I saw the dark expression on his face.

Rune didn't want to hear an apology from me. I was an assassin who had been sent here to kill him. Even though I'd decided against it, that didn't change the truth about who I was.

All I could do was give him a nod, then dash into the trees. The forest swallowed me whole.

16

RUNE

"What in fate's name was that about?" were the first words out of Lilia's mouth when I'd collected myself enough to step through the door. The scent of stew filled the room, but my appetite was shot now. I couldn't eat when I knew the guild had finally sent someone for me—someone I'd wanted to believe was too good to be one of them.

I heaved a tired sigh, thundered over to the table, and collapsed into an open chair. It was just so fucking disappointing. Frida's sweet smile, the light in her eyes when she gazed upon the world with pure delight. All of it was fake. Assassins didn't look at anything that way.

"You remember the Assassin's Guild?" I asked Ragnar.

His face instantly clouded over. "How could I forget? They used to be in league with the Mercenaries Guild. When I first visited the Isles a few decades ago, they chased me here and tried to make me pay my brother's debts. Why? What does that have to do with Frida?"

"I was in the guild before I came here."

"That's right. I always forget you were a member," Lilia said, frowning. "Sorry Rune. You're just nothing like the others I've met."

"Neither is Frida," I said quietly.

Ragnar straightened. "That sweet elven lass we just met? Surely she can't be."

I held up the ball of parchment she'd tossed to the ground, then passed it over to Ragnar. I'd read the words outside while she'd been collecting her pack from the cottage. It corroborated what she'd told me. This was her first assignment, and she'd originally come here thinking she had to steal a dragon.

I was more relieved than I should have been. When I'd caught her out there with a messenger owl, I'd braced myself for a fictionalized tale good enough for a Silva Sweetwater novel. And at first, that was all it had seemed to be. A sad story about her family provided a good excuse.

But then she'd gone to ground, and I'd read the note she'd left behind, and a part of me wanted to believe every word that came out of that pretty mouth.

Ragnar quickly read the message and loosed a low whistle. Grimacing, he passed it to Lilia. "Looks like they finally figured out a way to get around the island's magic."

I nodded. "If they send someone who doesn't know why they're coming here, it's the perfect trick. Of course, it's not easy to replicate. They needed someone who was new to the guild and didn't know better. Also someone willing to go on a nonsensical assignment. Who in their right mind thinks they can steal a bloody dragon?"

Lilia pursed her lips. "Do you think Frida believed she'd be successful?"

"From what she told me, it didn't matter. She was desperate enough to try."

"Why?" Lilia asked.

I ran a hand along the top of my head, sighing. "Her father is Erik's right-hand man. She's a Rurik. They're all guild members and always have been."

Lilia looked to Ragnar, who nodded. "They've been a part of the guild for a very long time. I'm surprised Frida is joining so late. Family members tend to join young. Too young, if you ask me."

I quickly filled them in on the rest of Frida's story. And as I recounted her words, an image of her tear-stained face flashed in my mind. My stomach twisted. Either she was an excellent actress, or she truly regretted ever considering a life in the guild.

After I'd told them what I knew, Ragnar frowned. "Rune, surely you don't mean for her to return to the guild empty-handed. We both know what they're like and the lengths they're willing to go to in order to get what they want."

"What are you trying to say?" Lilia asked, alarmed.

"If this is Frida's induction assignment, that means she's not an official member of the guild yet, which means she lives outside the bounds of their protection."

I shook my head. "Her father would never let Erik punish her in that way."

"You might be right," Ragnar conceded. "But I wouldn't be willing to stake gold on that. Would you?"

"You should tell her to stay here," Lilia said. "They won't let her join if she doesn't complete the assignment, so she has no reason to go back to Vilmar."

"They'll send someone else if she never returns," Ragnar said.

"That might be a long time from now. Like you said, they need a certain type of person to pull it off," she argued.

"They can't send someone with the intention of targeting Rune, but they could *certainly* send someone to search for a missing daughter. And *that* person might be a lot more difficult to deal with than Frida." Ragnar cocked his brow. "But I have an idea. You probably won't like it, though, darling."

"Oh, lovely. I always enjoy when you say things like that." Lilia shot him a flat stare.

Ragnar grinned, motioning both of us closer. "What if we simply use Erik's tricks against him?"

After Lilia and Ragnar returned to the inn for the night, I settled into my rocking chair with Moira curled in my lap. I absentmindedly stroked her fur, my mind spinning. Ragnar's plan was…well, it was fucking ridiculous. There was no other way to say it. It was as likely to succeed as I was to invite a hundred people into my house to make a mess of it.

A gust of wind barrelled against the house. It slipped through the cracks, bringing a chill to the air, despite the hearth-fire. Frowning, I stood, lifted Moira into my arms, and moved over to the window. The world outside had vanished, replaced by an impenetrable black wall.

My gut churned. The Elding was coming back, and Frida was out there in the thick of it.

I owed her nothing. Even if she hadn't realized it when she'd boarded that ship, she'd come here to kill me. And if Erik hadn't lied to her, she likely would have shot an arrow at my head on that very first night. She only hesitated now because I was no longer a faceless mark to her. She'd gotten to know me. She'd helped me save a woman's life.

Clenching my jaw, I grabbed my cloak from the hook beside the door and took off into the night. The temperature had dropped, and the harsh wind tunnelled through my garden. A fallen branch scraped along the ground, its leaves shuddering with a desperation to break free.

Stumbling forward, I hunted down the path I'd watched Frida take earlier and broke out into a run. The world was so dark, I struggled forward, but I knew these woods so well that I managed to stick to the path.

I had a feeling I knew where I'd find Frida. By this point, she'd have realized the storm was returning, and she would have sought the only shelter of which she was aware. That tree hollow might seem like a decent enough protection against a storm, but the Elding was no normal storm. The persistent wind and rain would force their way inside until it stole all her breath away.

"Frida!" I called out when I thought I was near enough to the tree for her to hear me. Everything was so dark. Only the vague shape of trunks and wild brush surrounded me, the darkness smudging everything else. "FRIDA!"

With the wind howling around me, I held myself still and listened for any sound that might indicate her direction. But would she even answer if she heard my voice? If I were her, I likely wouldn't.

If I were her, I'd be afraid of me.

I was an orc and a former member of a guild full of murderous assholes. I'd caught her in a lie, and she'd fled to get away from me. And now I was stalking around the woods, shouting for her with an axe strapped to my back. She'd probably think I'd come out here to stop her from returning to the guild.

The wind rustled the leaves by my feet, bringing with it a soft sound. "Rune?"

I whirled toward her voice and felt my way down the path. My outstretched hands met the rough bark of a redwood tree. Fingers wrapped around my ankle, tugging me down.

I knelt. Frida's hand slid up my side until it paused on my shoulder. "Rune, why are you here?"

"The storm's coming back," I said gruffly. "Didn't you realize?"

"Well, yes. That's why I'm inside the tree."

"It's not safe enough. I'm taking you back to the cottage."

A long moment of silence stretched between us, then she said, "You want me to come back?"

"I know you probably think I'm mad, but I can't let you stay out here during the storm. It's not right, no matter why you came here," I said.

Her hand stiffened on my shoulder. "I came here to steal your dragon. The other thing is inconsequential."

"Inconsequential?" I barked a laugh. "I daresay Erik won't agree when you return without my head."

"It's about time Erik learned he can't always have what he wants," she snapped.

A blast of wind hit me in the back, nearly knocking me into the tree. Bracing myself, I reached inside the hollow and found Frida's other hand. "We'll argue about this later. Right now, I need you to come with me."

"Rune," she whispered, tugging her hand away from me.

"Don't be so stubborn, Frida. If you stay out here, you could—"

"You shouldn't be helping me," she said, her voice a little louder—a little stronger—now. "I'm your enemy. My people, the guild—"

"The guild members aren't your people," I said firmly.

"Of course they are! I was born into it. The guild's ways run in my blood."

I shook my head. The bloody elf was more stubborn than I was.

Heavy droplets of rain tore through the canopy. A few landed on my arms, and pain lashed through me. Cursing beneath my breath, I leaned into the trunk and wound my arms around Frida's body. Then, despite knowing how much she would hate me for this, I tossed her over my shoulder.

A cry of alarm tore from her throat, but I ignored it. With her body tucked tightly against mine, I took off down the path, swatting stray branches aside. Wind and rain beat against me. The moments felt agonizingly long, like we'd been trapped fleeing this storm for hours. Eventually, the pale light from my cottage shone through the darkness. I stumbled toward it, clenching my jaw against the pain.

Just a little further. A few more steps, and we'd be out of the rain. But as I thundered toward my cottage, a numbness filled my head. It was too much. Far too much. I'd only been caught out like this a handful of times, but each one had brought me to my knees.

The world around me seemed to blur, my vision darkening at the edges.

We reached the door, and I kicked it open, stumbling into the safety of my cottage. Angry heat tore through me. Streaks of yellow filled my eyes, transforming the room into nothing more than a meaningless blob of light.

Gritting my teeth, I tried to be gentle when I lowered Frida, but my knees buckled. My leg thundered into the floor, jolting me. Frida's weight vanished from my shoulder. And then everything went black.

17

FRIDA

Rune was burning up. Sprawled across the timber floor of his cottage, he was completely unconscious. I leaned over him, examining his body. His trousers and his cloak seemed to be crafted from leather that had been treated with copious amounts of oil, which made them pretty water resistant. The material had taken the brunt of the rain, but enough had broken through the front of the cloak to drench his tunic.

Moira raced over, meowing furiously. Strands of her black hair littered the floor. She weaved back and forth, her ferocious little gaze locked on Rune's prone form.

"I'm sorry," I whispered. "This is my fault. He wouldn't be like this if he hadn't come looking for me."

Why had he come for me? It was completely nonsensical. If he had any wits about him, he would have left me to ride out the storm. I'd told him I planned to return to the guild and lie about his existence. If he'd left me alone, he could have rid his troubled mind of Erik once and for all.

But that could still happen. There was nothing stopping me from walking away now and finding a better hiding place. Nothing but my instinct to help him.

And the Elding.

I glanced at the door. Wind rattled the wood against the hinges, and the sound of the rain had built to a roar. Going outside now would be foolish, but even if the storm let up, I couldn't leave him like this.

Gently, I unhooked the front of his cloak and tugged it off his body. Then I sat back on my heels, wringing my hands. Through the thin, wet material of his tunic, I could already see his skin turning red. Really, I needed to remove the shirt. It was the best thing for him.

Heart pounding in my ears, I leaned over him and quickly unbuttoned the tunic before sliding the front of it off his shoulders. His muscular torso gleamed in the flickering hearth-light, and angry red welts marred his oak moss skin. Swallowing, I leapt to my feet, dashed into my bedroom, and grabbed one of the towels he'd provided for me.

When I returned to his side, Rune had awakened, though his eyes were slitted in pain. I patted his skin with the towel, trying my best to avoid pressing the welts too hard.

"Can you sit up?" I asked him.

"You don't need to fuss like this."

"I can try to pull the shirt out from under you, but I don't know how I'll manage with all your weight on it."

A strange smile curled his lips. "This might be the most ironic moment of my life. My assassin is trying to get me naked so she can save me from more pain."

"Don't get so excited," I scolded him. "I only want to get you topless. Now can you sit up or not?"

"All right. But I apologize ahead of time for the words that might come out of my mouth."

"I've lived in a guild-hall with a bunch of assassins for an entire year," I said dryly. "Nothing you can say would be worse than what they spouted on a daily basis."

That smile appeared again, and a flush of satisfaction warmed my chest. "Careful, I might take that as a challenge."

Rune palmed the floor beside him, and I slid my

hands along the curves of his shoulders to help keep him steady. With a pain-filled grunt, he shoved against the timber, conjuring a small gap. Quickly, I peeled the material out from under his body, and he thunked back onto the floor.

"Fucking fate." He closed his eyes, his breath coming out in short puffs. "That fucking hurt."

"I'm sorry. You'll feel better after I get your salve." I stood. "Wait here."

His low chuckle followed me to his bedroom door. "Do I really look like I'm going to wander away right now?"

A smile tickled my lips. Shaking my head, I went inside his room and took two tins from his salve collection. Back in the main room, he'd closed his eyes again. He was silent as I spread the salve across the wounds on his chest, which made it a lot easier. I had difficulty concentrating on what I was doing when he was staring up at me.

When I was done, I managed to get him on his feet. With his arm wrapped around my shoulder, we shuffled into his bedroom. I turned my back to him while he shucked off his trousers and climbed into bed.

"All right, you can turn around now," he said.

I moved to his side, fighting the urge to drape my hand across his forehead to check his temperature. "Do you need anything else?"

"Yes. I need you to not do what you're thinking of doing," he said. I opened my mouth to argue, but he cut me off. "I can tell by the look on your face. You're wondering if you should leave now, since I'd struggle to chase you. Don't do it, Frida. Stay."

"Why? What could possibly compel you to want me to stay?" My voice came out rough.

"I have an idea that could fix things for all of us. But you need to stay and hear me out."

I nibbled on my bottom lip, then said, "I don't see what could be better than my plan to return to the guild and tell Erik you're not here."

"You need to take him something, or he'll say you failed." Rune's eyes slid shut. "And then you'll get kicked out of the guild. Or worse. I know you don't want that."

"What could I possibly take him?"

"A dragon," Rune said.

I blinked. "*What?*"

"A dragon. His name is Eldi, and he's lived on this island for the past twenty odd years. It might take a little effort on your part to get him to trust you. But if you manage it, you can take him to Erik and say you never got the second assignment letter. You did what he asked, and now he has a dragon." Rune cracked open one eye. "Though you'll have to swear you'll help Eldi get out of there once you're fully inducted into the guild. Erik is a bastard who can never have a dragon under his command."

My heart pounded, shock punching me in the gut. When I spoke, my voice came out only as a whisper. "So you *do* have a dragon. You've had one this entire time?"

"No. He's not mine," Rune said gruffly. "I had a dragon once, and once was all I needed. I don't have it in me to bond with another. So if you want to convince him to help you, he's all yours. It just might not be easy."

My mind spun through everything he'd told me. I'd be a fool to think this could work. Erik had never sent me here for the dragon—that wasn't what he truly wanted. But how could he be certain I'd received his message? The Elding raged outside, drowning the island in wind and rain. It shouldn't be difficult to convince Erik that the owl had never reached me or that the parchment had been lost to the storm.

If I took him a dragon, I'd technically complete the original assignment. *That* wasn't failure. He'd *have* to make me a full member because I'd done the impossible for him. While I was at it, I could even say I'd never met an orc. I'd found the dragon all on my own. Erik would have to look elsewhere for Rune.

Rune was right. This could fix things for *everyone.*

Hope bloomed in my chest. I nodded and held out my hand. "It's a deal."

Rune chuckled, though he gently took my hand and shook it. "Don't get so excited. Like I said, it might not be easy."

The next morning, the cottage was empty, and the sound of splitting wood drifted in from the open front door. Rune had left a basket of bread on the table for me, though I suspected he'd had a good deal of it himself if the muddy footsteps leading to and from the table were any indication. Shaking my head, I took a chunk of the bread and poked my head outside.

Rune stood beside a pile of wooden logs, sweat curling across his bare, mottled chest. He heaved his axe into the air and brought the sharp end down on a log. It split in two, and he tossed the pieces into the growing pile. His taut muscles glistened in the morning sunlight slanting through the trees. Swallowing, I wandered over to him, noticing he'd already cleared up the broken section of his shed.

"Either you have an addiction to work or you

heal faster than anyone I've ever met," I said, giving him a flat stare. "Don't you need to rest?"

"Rest is for the wicked," he said, easing the head of his axe onto the ground and draping one arm across the handle. Fate, he looked incredible. Not that I cared, of course. I was just noticing. Most people would.

I cleared my throat. "Now that's just not true. After the night you had, no one would think you're *wicked* for taking the day off."

"Helga needs a new home, and the dwarves need a fence." Rocking back on his heels, he swiped the back of his arm across his forehead. "I'm not in bad enough shape to let them down by not doing my job."

I frowned. "If they knew what happened last night, I'm sure they'd understand. Let me—"

"You're not going to talk me out of it, but if you want to help, feel free to jump in," he said in a voice that brooked no argument. He was going to do this, even if every wound on his chest still looked angry and raw—which they did. And if I didn't help him, he'd have double the work. Last night, I'd agreed to carry on as his assistant while I tried to tame the dragon, and I'd meant it. If he didn't want to kick me out after what he'd learned about me, then I was happy to stay and leave a good mark on this island. And that meant helping him do whatever woodworking tasks needed doing.

I sighed. "All right. Where should I start?"

Rune motioned at the pile of split logs. "Get those inside the shop. We can't risk the wood getting wet if the storm decides to swing back around another time."

And so I nodded, squared my shoulders, and got to work.

~

The hardest, most physically exhausting work of my life consumed the next few days. Every morning just before dawn, Rune slammed his fist against my door with enough force that I was sure the wood would spring free of its hinges sooner rather than later. I threw on my clothes and padded out into the main room rubbing sleep from my eyes, only to find Rune was already outside hammering or sawing or muttering curses beneath his breath.

My glaring lack of skills initiated more than one debate about how I could possibly have the steady aim of an expert archer but manage to fumble a bag of nails. After one such argument, I spent at least an hour on my hands and knees, picking through the grass to find every nail I'd dropped. Other times, he praised my dogged insistence to toil away for the same long hours that he did. In fact, I remained on my feet for so long that my eyes slammed shut within seconds of my head hitting the pillow every night.

Several days after Rune had rescued me from the redwood tree, I sat cross-legged on the dwarven farm, erecting a section of their new fence while Rune was back at the cottage prepping timber beams for Helga's replacement home. The children were out playing in the garden while Arvid and his partner were tending to their horses. It was a peaceful late-spring afternoon. Birds perched in the drooping branches overhead, filling the air with their high-pitched orchestra. The Elding had not shown its face since that fateful night. Clear skies and peaceful breezes had chased it away, and the sun's warmth caressed the back of my neck.

I hummed to myself, proud of how much progress I'd made in such a short time. About a quarter of the fence was already completed, though I'd nearly run out of wood. Still, at this rate, I'd finish well within the two-week time period we'd promised the dwarves.

Arvid wandered over with a steaming mug in his hand. "Thought you might like a cup of tea while you work, but I didn't account for how hot it is out here. Summer is well and truly on its way."

I set the beam of wood down, smiling. "I don't mind how warm it is. A mug of tea sounds lovely right now. Thank you, Arvid."

He eagerly handed it over, the bells in his beard chiming. "I hope you like it. There's a lot more where that came from." Shifting on his feet, he cleared his throat. "And I, ah…well, I'd be happy to keep your mug filled with as much as you can drink."

A knowing smile spread across my face. "What is it, Arvid? Would you like me to change something about the fence?"

"Oh no!" His eyes went wide. "I love the fence. It's perfect. It's just…while you were here yesterday, I went to see how Rune was getting on with Helga's house, and he mentioned you're an excellent archer. One of the best, in fact, he said."

For an odd reason I couldn't quite identify, my heart lurched. "Rune actually said that to you?"

"Oh yes. He said he had every faith you'll do well in woodworking because you know how to dedicate yourself to learning a skill."

"Well, that's…" Surprisingly complimentary. Rune had been his grumpy self these past few days. He'd been so involved with his work that he had little time and energy at the end of the day to do more than exchange a few pleasantries before heading off to bed. My own bone-aching weariness welcomed the early nights, especially since it meant I'd already torn through two of the romance novels he 'accidentally' owned.

At times, I'd wondered if he might regret offering me the position. The two of us barely talked, even over dinner.

"Anyway." Arvid rocked back on his heels, nervously twisting his hands. "One of my girls keeps pestering me about archery, but the thing is, it's not really something taught down in the Deep, where I grew up. Now I know you're busy right now, but once you have some free time, I was hoping you might be willing to consider showing her some tricks. In exchange for some tea, of course. I mean, if you might possibly have any inkling of a willingness to maybe—"

"Of course I'll teach your daughter, Arvid," I cut in softly, partly to put him out of his rambling misery and partly because my chest seemed to expand at the thought of teaching someone else to use a bow and arrow, the same way my mother had taught me. An ache went through me, remembering her smile.

"What? You wouldn't mind?" He stood up a little straighter.

"I would love to. In fact, I'd be honored."

He clapped his hands, his eyes brightening with enough light that they could rival the sun. "Oh, thank you, Frida. Thank you, thank you, thank you. I can't wait to tell her. She'll be so excited!"

"Well, go on then." I grinned. "As long as you don't mind me using a daily hour of fence building time, you can even tell her we'll start tomorrow."

"Absolutely!" he exclaimed. And then he was off, bustling toward his cottage with his bells jingling wildly.

"That was kind of you," came a rumbling voice from behind me.

Stomach twisting, I turned toward said voice to find Rune walking up and down the length of my fence, poking at every beam, like the whole thing might collapse against the slightest bit of pressure.

"It's not kindness. He's paying me in tea."

His lips quirked up in the corners. "Yes, you're very greedy with your demands for tea and cheese."

"And books," I added.

He arched a brow. "I couldn't help but notice you're already done with two. I've only got one more. After that, you'll have to try another genre."

"Or maybe you could just admit you like romance novels and get a few more." Grinning up at him, I brushed the wood shavings from my palms and stood.

"Those were accidental purchases, and—"

"*One* might be accidental," I said, taking a step

toward him. "Two is a little harder to believe, but I'd let it slide. *Three*, however…Well, that seems pretty damn purposeful to me."

A full-on grin filled his face. "I'm afraid I've never read a romance book in my life. Sorry to disappoint you, sunshine."

A heady warmth filled my chest, then skated up my neck and into my face. My eyes caught on his, on the rich brown of his irises. They were the color of freshly tilled earth, of the timber beams he'd dedicated his life to sanding and polishing and building his entire world around. He was this forest, and the forest was him. And not for the first time in the past few days, I had the sudden urge to reach out and feel the warmth of his skin.

Instead, I cleared my throat and looked away. "That's okay. I'm sure I'll like the other books in your collection."

"Well, you still have one romance novel left. You can start reading it tonight after we get home from visiting Eldi."

My heart leapt into my throat. "The dragon? Today's the day?"

Rune had wanted to make headway on his work before taking me to meet the dragon, and I hadn't complained. He was doing me a favor with this, and deep down, I knew I didn't deserve his help. So I'd put my head down and had done what he'd asked, getting lost in the work myself.

But it was time. Today, I would set my sights on a dragon for the very first time, and I didn't know whether I should be excited or afraid. Maybe a bit of both.

18

FRIDA

The island was much larger than I'd been made to believe. Either the guild had lied to me (again) or they had insufficient information. Most likely, it was the latter. Before we'd left Rune's cottage, we'd packed a satchel full of snacks and filled up our waterskins. Two hours later, with my forehead coated in sweat, I understood why Rune had been so insistent on making preparations for the hike.

North of the dense forest, several craggy mountains reached for the late afternoon sky like gnarled fingers. Tall, swaying grass rippled across the knot of foothills beneath them, scented with the aroma of milkweed and…was that sulfur?

Rune slowed when he'd noticed I'd halted on the dirt path that cut across the foothills. My gaze had locked on the nearest mountain and the slant of a cave opening cut into the side of it. From within, an orange light pulsed.

"Are you afraid?" Rune asked.

"I don't know," I whispered. "Should I be?"

"As far as I know, Eldi has never harmed anyone. He likes to be left alone and might refuse to engage with us. But he's never roasted a visitor."

I cut my eyes toward Rune. "Kind of like you, then."

"You're right. And maybe that's my mistake. It'd certainly make folk leave me alone."

I smiled at him.

His brow furrowed. "What?"

"I think you secretly like having visitors. You just refuse to admit it to anyone, even to yourself."

He shook his head. "The words 'delusional' and 'assassin' are never a good combination."

A pang went through my heart, and after sucking in a deep breath, I started down the path again. Rune erased the distance between us in one stride and fell into step beside me. Out of the corner of my eye, I saw him looking at me, but I didn't give him the satisfaction of looking back.

"Which part annoyed you?" he asked. "Delusional or assassin?"

"Does it matter?"

"It really does." A beat passed. "If Erik accepts

your story, aren't you hoping he'll let you become a full member of the guild so you can be with your family?"

"That's the long and short of it, yes."

"Then you'll be an assassin, Frida, whether you want to think of yourself as one or not," he said softly.

I clenched my jaw. His words cut through me, mostly because he was right. The entire reason we were on this path was so that I could return to the guild without consequences. He was helping me *become* the very thing I wanted to pretend I wasn't.

"Maybe I plan to ask for thieving assignments," I said, nodding to myself. I'd never heard of Erik allowing members to dictate the type of assignments they took on, but maybe I could convince him. A dragon was an incredible prize, after all.

"I don't think you need me to explain how unlikely that is," Rune said. "It's time for you to deal with the fact you'll have to assassinate."

I came to a sudden stop again and whirled to face him. "I thought you wanted to help me with this."

A long stretch of silence followed, Rune's chestnut gaze searching my face. "I do want to help you, Frida. But when I look at you, I don't see one of them. I see a girl who'd be far better off staying on this island and starting a life she would love. I think if you go back to the guild, you'll be miserable. And beyond that, it'll change you."

"You don't know me, Rune," I whispered up at him, my heart pounding against my ribs. "This is what I want."

Sighing, he stepped back and motioned down the path. "After you, then. The dragon's cave is just up ahead."

I nodded tersely and moved past him. Rune didn't understand—*he couldn't*. As much as I liked to tease him about his solitude, he truly did enjoy his time alone. To him, my desperate need to feel a part of something probably seemed nonsensical.

It didn't help that Arvid's request had brought back a flood of memories. My mother had shown me how to shoot an arrow. I remembered the way she'd praised me during our sessions, loving me fiercely until the day I'd run away. And then her illness had killed her. I hadn't even been there to hold her hand at the end of it. Even now, I still grieved for those final months I'd lost with her, just because I hadn't been able to deal with the truth of who I was.

The path wound up the hill, leading to a rockier stretch that curled up the side of the mountain. About a quarter of the way up, a large cavern mouth yawned to our right. The dragon sat just inside the entrance, perched on his haunches. His spiked tail curled around enormous paws tipped in talons.

My breath fled from my lungs. Sunlight slanted into the cave, illuminating his glittering black scales. His head swooped to the side as he snuffed at the air, his muscular body so broad and tall that I suddenly felt inexplicably small. I had never seen anything like him, and my knees weakened at the sight. A low grumble spilled from his spiked mouth.

"Whoa, Eldi." Rune inched in front of me, his hands outstretched. He gazed up at the dragon with an ease that suggested he'd come here a time or two before. "It's Rune, remember? And this is Frida. She's an elven lass from the mainland, and she's come here to ask you for help."

Eldi snuffed again, then turned his head away.

"Can he understand you?" I whispered.

"He's a dragon. Of course he can understand me."

Eldi shifted further to the side, fully turning his back on us. His tail sliced across the ground and plumes of dust filled the air. Rune edged back a few steps, his body still a shield against the dragon. And then a moment later, the dragon was gone, vanishing into the depths of the cave.

"Hmm," I said. "It doesn't seem like he could understand you."

"He understood me just fine. The problem is, he doesn't want to help you," Rune said.

I frowned. "What, he decided, just like that?"

"I warned you it might be difficult."

"But he didn't even give me a chance to ask him." I squared my shoulders, calling upon my hopeful determination that had gotten me this far. "I'll just have to follow him and try again."

I started toward the cave, but Rune grabbed my arm and hauled me back behind him. "Don't do that. This is his home, and he's basically slammed the front door in our faces. You can't force your way inside and expect him to change his mind. You'll have to come back tomorrow and hope he'll consider listening then."

"But—"

"I told you it'd be hard and that it might take time." His eyes softened as he caught the look of despair I knew I wore. "If you keep trying, I'm sure you can win him over. You won me over, didn't you?"

A fluttering went through my stomach. "Did I?"

He chuckled. "Well, for the most part. I still don't think you could draw a fence if your life depended on it."

A heady warmth curled through my belly. And that was when I realized one of us had stepped toward the other—or maybe we both had. Only a slip of air filled the space between us, and his full lips and gleaming tusks were only inches away from my mouth. A wild thought flashed through my mind: an image of Rune pressing his body against mine, gently caressing my neck with his lips.

A delicious tremor went through me, heating me up in places where I'd not felt warmth in far too long.

Fuck.

Swallowing, I dragged my gaze away from him. I couldn't think these kinds of thoughts. Not about Rune. Not about anyone ever again. It was one thing to ignore the guild's rules and read a novel, drink some ale, or dance to a lovely bard's tune. It was quite another to climb into bed with the orc they'd sent me here to hunt.

I shook away those thoughts.

"I suppose we should head back," I said, my voice more strained than it had any right to be. "I just need to do something first."

I shrugged the satchel off my shoulder and pulled out the cheese I'd packed inside. Then, without daring to glance at Rune, I placed it on the ground just inside the cave's entrance. The dragon might not think much of me now, but if there was one thing I knew, it was that Arvid's cheese could please anyone.

It was my night to cook. After every gruesome detail about my truth had come out, I'd insisted that Rune let me do a bit more around the cottage to earn my keep. So we took turns preparing dinner now. The night before, he'd rustled up roasted pork, along with some fresh bread and greens dripping in butter. And when I'd asked him if there was anything in particular he wanted tonight, he'd vanished out the door without comment.

An hour had passed since he'd left, so I'd gotten started on stewing some barley I'd found stashed in his cupboard. Other than a sack of potatoes, there wasn't much else by way of food, at least that I could find. By the time I'd begun to consider leaving the pot over the hearth-fire to go in search of some mushrooms, Rune threw open the door and strode in with a line of fresh cod tossed over his shoulder.

"You all right making this?" he asked without preamble, tossing the fish onto the table.

I eyed him, still stirring the barley. "Did you just go catch some fish?"

"Of course. Where did you think I went?"

"Since you left without a word, I thought you might have decided the dragon had the right idea.

Maybe you went in search of your own cave to hide away in."

"Tempting," he said. "I think I'll wait until after you cook me that fish, though."

"Keep talking like that, and I'll throw this barley into a bowl and call it a day."

"Go ahead." His lips curled in the corners. "I know where you hid the rest of the cheese. Keep me hungry, and I'll gladly eat the whole damn lot of it."

I shot him a mock pout. "I didn't *hide* the cheese."

"You moved it from my food cupboard."

"I just thought it'd be better off in my room. You know, so that I don't disturb you again when I need a midnight snack."

Rune crossed the room, bringing with him the scent of salt and brine. As he drew closer, I noticed the droplets of water curling down his skin. His tunic was damp, the material clinging to his torso and defining every ridge of his chest. The pulse in my neck thrummed.

"Why do you insist on getting wet all the time when all it does is hurt you?" Sighing, I released the wooden spoon. "At this rate, you'll run out of salve soon."

"I went fishing in the sea, Frida. The salt water doesn't harm me," he said.

"Oh, right." My eyes skated across his wet clothes, heat curling through my stomach. In the days since it had last rained, his welts had mostly healed. And looking at him now, my fingers tensed, as if recalling the hard planes of his body when I'd applied the salve.

I cleared my throat, and Rune's eyes searched mine, like he could read the errant thoughts in my head.

"Are you sure you want to go back to that place?" he asked. Again.

"Yes, Rune. I'm sure." I turned back to the barley. It had congealed into a sticky mess that looked about as appealing as a bowl of mud. It was a good thing Rune had gone fishing, or we really would be dining on my last wheel of cheese tonight.

"All right, Frida." He sighed. "In that case, I've got something to show you after dinner. It'll help with Eldi." A pause. "But I need you to make a promise. No one can know about this, least of all Erik or anyone else who's a part of the guild. Not even your brother."

Curiosity prickled the back of my neck, and I turned to him with a raised brow. "Consider me intrigued."

Rune pointed at the fish. "Food first. Gift

second. If I'm going to share my secrets, I'd like to eat something that doesn't look like mud soup."

I grinned. "Fair enough."

After dinner, Rune and I sat beside the fire with Moira stretched across the floor by our feet. While I'd cleaned up, he'd disappeared into his room and returned with a small burlap sack. He dropped it on the table between us and steepled his hands beneath his chin, an expectant expression on his face.

"Any idea what that is?" he asked.

"I assume it's Galdur sand of some variety." I eyed him. "Fildur sand, for fire?"

"And what would make you think that?"

"Dragons have an affinity for fire. So do orcs. It's why you're able to bond with them without their magic consuming you."

"It's a good guess," he said with a nod. "But this is not any of the four elemental sands that most folk are aware of. In fact, scholars have fought hard to keep this one's existence a secret."

I sat up a little straighter. "You're saying there's a fifth sand?"

"I'm saying there are several sands that aren't

common knowledge. There's probably even more that scholars have yet to discover." He pointed at the little bag. "This one is called Hugur sand. It gives power over the mind. As I'm sure you can imagine, it would be incredibly dangerous in the wrong hands."

My gut churned as the implication of his words sank in. "You're saying there's a sand that can control people's thoughts?"

"That is one use for it, yes."

"You have an entire bag of it," I whispered.

"Trust me, Frida. I have never used this sand against anyone. I gathered it years ago and have kept it safe ever since," he said.

My heart pounded as I looked at the burlap sack. "Surely you don't intend for me to use it against a dragon. To control his thoughts so he'll help me?"

"Absolutely not," he said, narrowing his eyes. "And if I thought you'd commit that kind of atrocity, I'd never have shown this to you. It's to communicate with him and understand his wishes. That's all."

"Oh." I sat back in the chair, and it rocked beneath me. "So I could use it to read his thoughts?"

"Hmm, not exactly. You'd speak to him, and he'd speak back to you in your mind. It would help you learn if there was something you could offer him in exchange for his help."

I nodded. It made sense. "This is an incredible bit of magic you've discovered, Rune. The ability to communicate with animals…well, that could be life-changing. You could do so much for this island if you used it more."

He shook his head, sighing. "I'm hesitant to use it, especially knowing Erik is still looking for me after all these years. I'd never want him to get his hands on it."

For a moment, all I could do was stare at him, the crackle of the hearth the only sound. And then I cleared my throat, unsure if I should speak my thoughts aloud and risk him changing his mind about sharing this magic with me.

"I don't understand why you're telling me this. I'm part of the guild. Aren't I exactly the kind of person you want to hide this magic from?"

Rune folded his arms, leaned back in his chair, and gave me a long-considering look. "I see you, Frida, whether or not you see yourself yet."

I flushed. "What's that supposed to mean?"

He looked at me, and I looked at him, and an inscrutable expression crossed his face. Sighing, he ran a hand along the strong curves of his jaw.

"Maybe one day you'll understand." Rune rose,

pushing up from his chair. "For now, take that sand. You can visit Eldi as often as you like, just so long as you make good progress on the fence every day."

"Wait, you're not going with me next time?"

He shook his head. "There's too much work to do on Helga's house for me to hike to the cave and back every day. The Elding has moved on now, so it's safe. Just make sure you tell me when you go so I can come for you if need be."

"But Rune—"

"Good night, Frida." He knelt and gathered his cat into his arms, then vanished through his bedroom door. Swallowing, I stared after him, my heartbeat thundering through me. He was right to be so dismissive. Already, he'd done so much. Still, it stung.

He wanted to keep his distance from me, that much was clear. And it was probably for the best. Because after I tamed this dragon, I'd leave the Floating Forest and never look back. Saying goodbye would be hard enough as it was. Deepening our strained alliance into friendship would only make it harder.

19

FRIDA

The next few days passed in a blur. As soon as the rising sun washed the world in pale orange light, I was out the door with a new bundle of wood in my arms. The morning hours passed quickly as I worked on Arvid's fence, and despite the callouses roughening up my palms, the work had a steadying effect on me.

After lunch, I always spent an hour with Arvid's daughter. Even at eight years of age, Eydis was a bright, determined girl who handled the bow like someone who'd already spent hours attempting to learn the tricks of the trade herself. As eager as she was, it didn't take long to teach her the basics. Another week or two wasn't long enough to turn her into an expert, of course, but I could leave her with enough skills that she could eventually sharpen her base knowledge into something fierce.

The afternoon was my favorite part of the day—and my least. Every day, I made the long trek to the cave, where I attempted to converse with the dragon. The first afternoon, all I got was another round of huffing in my face before Eldi turned his back on me and stalked into the darkness again. Even with the new Hugur sand, his mind was a blank wall of nothingness to me.

The following day, I actually got something from him. When I asked what kind of things he liked, I had the overwhelming sensation of looking out at a long stretch of sea, the water glimmering beneath a high summer sun. But just as soon as the image filled my mind, it vanished.

On the fourth or fifth day—it was difficult to keep track with the long hours I spent on my feet—I doggedly trudged along the path to the cave again. This time, Eldi was curled in the swaying grass that spread across the foothills beneath the shadow of the mountain. Butterflies danced around his head, and birds whistled in the distance. As his powerful breath blew the surrounding grass, I had to pause for a moment and bask in his majestic aura. His glimmering black scales. That proud glint in his eye. Even though I'd seen him several times now, the awe had yet to fade.

As I approached him, I tossed a few grains of sand into my mouth and washed it down with some water. Instantly, I sensed something different from him—something *more* than what I'd felt before.

It still wasn't quite words, but I swore I could feel emotions pulsing from him, or the brush of his soul against mine. He seemed...sad. And lonely. And a bit lost, like he didn't quite know how to turn his sadness into joy. Perhaps he didn't even know what he wanted.

With his emotions churning through me, I decided I wouldn't mention my own troubles today. Instead, I sat cross-legged nearby and brought out the snacks I'd packed in my satchel: a heel of bread, some dried meat, and a small chunk of cheese. I'd gone through most of what Arvid had given me.

I put together a sandwich for the dragon and tossed it to him. He caught the food in mid-air, his mighty teeth slashing down on it. Smiling, I ate the half I'd left for myself and considered my next steps. I was nowhere near winning Eldi over, but he seemed less outwardly suspicious of me now. Maybe all he needed was patience and a lot of time —time I didn't really have.

"You have a lovely cave," I called out to him. "And it's lovely out here on the hills, too. Do you know where else is lovely?"

No answer, though I didn't expect one just yet.

"Oakwater." I let a beat pass. "The folk there are so kind and welcoming of outsiders. And wouldn't you know it, they're also very interested in dragons. I'm sure you know Lilia and her dragon, Reykur. He's your brother, isn't he?"

Again, no response, though another pulse of sadness brushed against me.

"Anyway, the folk of Oakwater love Reykur. I'm sure they'd love you, too."

Over the past few days, I'd had no time to head into Oakwater to ask around about dragons, but Arvid and his daughter had been more than happy to oblige my curiosities. Apparently, both Lilia and her dragon friend were well-loved on the island. Here, they didn't fear the beasts. Most of the villagers were even aware that Eldi lived nearby, but he was so reclusive, they rarely thought of him.

I couldn't imagine how lonely he must be. According to every legend I'd heard, dragons weren't meant for solitude. They suffered with loneliness just as much as folk.

Eldi huffed, and that aching sense of loneliness brushed against me once again.

I nodded. "I understand how it feels to be

lonely. Before I came here, I lived alone for a very long time. Really, it's how I ended up coming to this island."

A dash of fear followed the sense of loneliness. I cocked my head, trying to understand what that could mean. Was the dragon afraid of the towns-people? But why? Surely they'd never done something to frighten him. If they had, I was certain I would have heard about it. In fact, there were rumors the villagers were considering starting up the Dragon Festival again to *celebrate* the mighty beasts. Arvid and his partner, Mellor, were beside themselves with excitement about it.

"Should I swallow some more sand? I've still got plenty," I said, lifting the burlap sack. "Would that help you tell me what's wrong?"

The dragon rose, spread his wings, and gazed up at the clear cerulean sky. A wash of fear rolled over me, like angry waves at sea. And suddenly, I understood. Why Eldi was here. Why he remained hidden away in his cave. Somehow, against all odds, the dragon had succumbed to a fear of flying. He was stuck on the ground, as if his wings had been cast into stone.

I loosed a sigh of sorrow for him, but also one of resignation. Because as much as I needed him, I couldn't bear the thought of forcing him to fly. I'd have to find another solution to my problem. What that could possibly be, I had no idea. But I wouldn't cause terror in the heart of this gorgeous creature just to get what I wanted.

I sat with him for a while longer, regaling him with stories of my time back in the Kingdom of Edda. Even though I couldn't hear his voice in my mind, his emotions remained with me. He seemed to take pleasure in listening to me talk, and by the time the sky bled pink, I realized I was reluctant to leave. I enjoyed his company just as much as he enjoyed mine. Being with him reminded me a lot of Stella, and out of everything back home, I missed her most.

After I climbed to my feet, I gingerly walked toward him. Dragons were known to burn anything that touched them, but Eldi had been sitting in the grass for hours, and the flames had yet to devour it all. Timidly, I reached toward him. With a low rumble in his throat, he lowered his snout and brushed it against my fingers.

His skin was rough and hot, but painless. Smiling, I ran my palm along his scales. He leaned into me, and a deep, soul-settling sigh poured out of him, rustling my clothes. A sense of peace rolled toward me as we touched. The magic of the Hugur sand seemed to tug my soul toward his, filling my veins with incandescent hope and belonging. Tears pricked the corners of my eyes. For a moment, we just stood there, taking comfort in each other in a way I never would have dreamed.

"I'll be back tomorrow," I whispered to him.

~

"How did it go?" Rune asked the moment I stepped through the door. He'd left it propped open, and the evening forest filled the cottage with its orchestra of chattering squirrels and buzzing insects. A soft breeze rolled in, and the hearth-fire's flames lengthened and spit sparks into the air.

"The Hugur sand finally worked a little. I could feel some things from him," I said, tossing my satchel into its regular spot beside the door and toeing off my boots. "Emotions only, though. Still no words."

Tonight was Rune's turn to cook, and he'd already set bowls of vegetable stew and platters of salted fish and bread on the table. Steam still curled from the food. He must have seen me coming and hurried to have dinner plated up as soon as I walked through the door.

A flame of affection burned through me.

"That's good. It's progress," Rune said, settling into his chair at the dinner table.

I padded over to him, leaning down to scratch

Moira's chin on the way. "You might not say that when you hear what I've learned."

As we dug into the food, I told Rune about my day. When I reached the part about the dragon's fear of flying, an incredulous expression crossed his face. I hurried to tell him I'd figure out another solution, but he shook his head.

He waved a slice of bread at me. "Frida 'Determined' Rurik has given up that easily? I'm sure you can convince him to listen to you."

"I would rather be Frida 'Sympathetic' Rurik," I said with a frown. "Rune, the dragon is afraid of flying to Oakwater, which wouldn't even take him more than a few minutes. There's no way I'm asking him to fly all the way back to the mainland."

He searched my gaze. "So what are you going to do? Stay here instead?"

"No. I suppose I'll just have to return empty-handed. It'll be fine, I'm sure. I can make something up."

"Right. We're back to that, then." Rune sighed. "At least try to help Eldi before you go."

"Help him how?"

"With a little patience and a lot of encouragement, I bet you can help him fly to the village. If he can master that, he can visit anytime, and then he won't be so lonely anymore. It'd be good for him."

I chewed on my fish, examining Rune's face for

any sign he was joking. But he looked deadly serious.

"You want me to convince a dragon that his fears are meaningless?"

"Meaningless? No. But he can overcome them enough to reach the village, don't you think? And then you can return to the guild and tell Erik whatever you think is best."

I squinted at him. "You don't sound particularly happy about that plan."

Rune leaned back in his chair, eyeing me with an intensity that seared me. "You and the dragon have a lot in common, Frida. You said you could feel the loneliness rolling off of him, like a wave that might pull you under. Well, I've felt that same thing from you. It's not a feeling I'd wish upon anyone. And so if you believe the guild will make you happy, then you should go back to them. Because you deserve to be happy. Same as anyone else."

I swallowed, my heart pounding. "Are *you* happy?"

He blinked, like he was surprised I'd ask. "Happy?"

"Yes, Rune. Happy. Sometimes it seems like this island is exactly where you want to be. Other times, it seems like you find everything around you either annoying or downright awful."

"Nothing about Oakwater annoys me, and it's certainly not awful. There's nowhere in this godforsaken world I'd rather live," he said quietly. "But no, that doesn't mean I'm happy."

"And what would make you happy, Rune?"

A long stretch of silence followed. My heart beat wildly against my ribs, and I felt a desperate need to know exactly what would make Rune smile. *Permanently*. But I was also afraid to hear the answer. It felt like I was standing on the edge of a cliff, and his words might push me over.

Rune rubbed his jaw, looking away. "I'll be happy just doing my best to make this village a better place."

"But you already do that," I insisted. "Every damn day."

"The thing I truly want is never going to happen, Frida, and I accepted that a long time ago," he said.

"And what is that?" I asked. I knew I should let it go, but I couldn't. Rune had everything he said he wanted. He'd built the home of his dreams, he had the job he loved, and he was surrounded by people he cared for and respected.

But there was something missing. I could see it in the hollowness of those rich brown eyes.

A muscle feathered in his jaw. "I suppose I want the same thing most folk do. When I first came here, I pictured my house the way it is now. With a cat and a hearth and my woodworking shop, all surrounded by the most majestic trees I've ever seen. But there was something else in my picture, too—or someone else, specifically. I always imagined I'd spend my life with a companion by my side. Someone I could share my days with. Someone who saw me for what I am and loved me in spite of it. But I'm a hard person to love, so I gave up on that dream years ago."

"Rune," I whispered, my heart throbbing painfully in my chest. "You're not a hard person to love at all."

"Oh yeah?" He arched a brow. "Well, I'm still alone out here, aren't I?"

"Only because you haven't met the right person."

"Who's going to love a big orc with tusks, awkward social skills, and blood on his hands? I'll tell you who. No one." With a sigh, he stood and collected the dirty bowls. "You must be tired, so I'll clean up. I've put a book for you on your bed."

I frowned, but didn't argue. Rune was done with this conversation, and I could hardly blame him. I'd felt the same way about companionship lately, especially after I'd made my vows to the guild. I'd always been drawn to romance novels because I yearned to experience the all-consuming passion that happened between the pages. Even though I'd never felt those emotions myself, the books had given me hope. Hope that one day I might find the kind of love I'd only ever read about.

But I never had. And now I never would.

Rune would, though. I was certain of it. All those things he hated about himself? He was wrong about them. His dark past didn't matter, not compared to all the good he'd done since then. And while he *was* awkward at times, he was also kind, and funny, and generous to a fault.

He was also incredibly handsome. The fact he thought he wasn't, just because of his tusks, was ludicrous. If anything, they gave him an edge.

My heart dropped into my stomach as an intrusive thought pushed its way to the surface of my mind. One I'd been trying very hard to ignore.

I *liked* Rune.

No, it was more than that. I was pretty sure I was falling for him.

20

FRIDA

The next morning, I felt like I had to tiptoe around the cottage to avoid the feelings that had sprung free last night, worried I'd step right into another trap of them. Every time I looked at Rune, I felt ensnared again. And when he passed me a mug of tea across the table, I could have sworn his eyes were burrowing into my mind and reading my thoughts. I couldn't possibly bear the thought of him knowing I had feelings for him. My pesky emotions needed to get a grip. This thing between us—a very one-sided thing, that much was abundantly clear—could go nowhere. Rune had never shown even an ounce of interest in me that way, and even if he had, I'd sworn a vow of celibacy.

More importantly, I had to leave this island soon.

Still, that knowledge didn't stop me from staring at his powerful, calloused hands as he hauled the door open to go to work. An image rose in my mind of those hands wrapped around my thighs, and I let out a strangled noise. Frowning, Rune looked over his shoulder at me, his broad shoulders outlined by the sun's morning light.

"Everything all right, Frida?" he asked, my name curling off his tongue.

"Yes, fine," I said, brushing invisible crumbs off the front of my tunic.

He squinted at me. "If you're sure…"

"Very sure," I chirped.

A beat passed. "Are you going to visit Eldi this afternoon?"

"That's the plan." I'd mulled over Rune's words from the night before, and I'd come to a decision. Eldi did need my help. He clearly wished for the skies, but fear kept him grounded. I would try to get him airborne, if only for his sake. And if he was willing to fly to the mainland after that, I'd welcome his help. But *only* if he had conquered his fear. I wouldn't push him beyond that.

"Good. I'll come with you," Rune said with a nod.

I swallowed. As much as a part of me yearned

for his company, the other part—the part that couldn't stop imagining how it would feel to have him kiss me—wanted to run screaming in the other direction. I'd planned to avoid spending time alone with him until I had to leave. But this would be a two-hour trek, then two hours back. That was a lot of time with just the two of us. Alone.

A lot of time where I'd have to force myself to ignore my blossoming feelings.

"Are you sure?" I asked. "I thought you were too busy with Helga's house build to spend an entire afternoon hiking to the mountains and back."

He smiled. "The villagers saw how much work needed doing, and they've all chipped in to help. I tried to tell them I could handle it myself, but they've insisted. So it'll be done in no time."

"Really?" I smiled back. "That's so lovely of them, Rune."

"They're good folk. I should have known they'd be eager to help in any way they could."

This place. These people. Now I understood why Rune wanted to protect them, beyond even what the magic could do.

The *magic*.

Suddenly, I understood what I must do. I didn't have to deliver Erik a dragon, and I certainly didn't have to return with my first kill notched into my belt. All we needed was for Erik to believe that the magic of this place had held firm against his machinations. He needed to think his loophole hadn't worked. That there was no way for someone in the guild to reach this island, no matter what tricks he tried, which meant he'd have to give up his quest of ever finding Rune. He had to believe there was no hope.

I shook my head, smiling. How had I not seen it before? It was the best solution for everyone. When I returned to the guild, I would tell Erik I'd never stepped foot on these shores. The magic had stopped me.

That afternoon, Rune and I made the journey to Eldi's cave on two pairs of tired feet. Despite the volunteers assisting with Helga's build, Rune wore weariness like a heavy cloak, and my muscles ached from my days spent building Arvid's fence. This past week had involved more physical labor than I'd ever done until now. Still, neither of us complained. We walked in a companionable silence, our elbows occasionally brushing. Every time the edge of his sleeve touched mine, I had to steel my spine and focus my gaze on the path ahead. I refused to let him see how much I wanted to turn an unintentional graze into some-thing far more.

After a time, I couldn't bear the silence any longer. "What's your favorite thing in the world, Rune?"

I thought he might scowl or grumble at the abrupt question, but he cocked his head and furrowed his brow as if he were seriously consid-ering his answer. "Your drawing of Arvid's fence."

I snorted a laugh. "Well, it *is* a very good draw-ing, if I do say so myself. I bet you could probably sell it for a trunk full of gold."

"Hmm. Or perhaps I should send it to the acad-emy, so the art students can study it in great detail. They might learn something from your scribbles." He gently elbowed me. "Though now that I've heard you snort when you laugh, I might have to change my answer."

My lips spread into a smile so wide my cheeks ached. "Really, though, what's your favorite thing? Give me a serious answer this time."

His eyes locked on mine. He opened his mouth, then snapped it shut. And then, with an expedi-tious clearing of his throat, he answered, "I suppose I'd have to say Moira."

"Aww. You really do love that bundle of fluff. I can't wait to tell Arvid your answer. Who will then tell Mellor, who will pass it on to Helga. And then the whole village will find out you're as mushy as a bowl of barley."

He grunted in response. "Don't get carried away now. What's yours?"

"Oh, I couldn't possibly choose. I love my horse, and I think about her all the time. I wish I'd been able to bring her with me. And I adore my cottage back home. Oh, I can't forget about purple lilies, and cheese, and the way the sky looks at sunset, and romance novels, and dancing in the rain, and the feel of the grass beneath my bare feet, and the redwoods on this island, and—" I stopped, catching the amusement in his eyes. "What?"

"I thought we were asking each other about our favorite *thing*," he said, elbowing me again. "If I hadn't stopped you just now, I think you could have kept going all day."

"There's a certain kind of joy in letting yourself love," I said.

His face darkened. "Joy and pain."

"Love doesn't have to be painful." Though I was starting to think it might. I couldn't remember a time when love had caused me anything but grief. Still, I wanted to believe there was a way for it to be better. Silva Sweetwater seemed to think so, anyway.

"And sometimes, the pain is inevitable." Sighing, he motioned ahead. "It looks like your new friend has come out to meet us."

Indeed, Eldi had ventured even further beyond his cave than the day before. He sat squarely on the path at the base of the foothills, his tail swishing through the grass. As we approached, he lowered his head and extended it toward me, as if he were asking for a pat.

And so of course I had to indulge him. Grinning, I scratched beneath his chin, and his body hummed against my fingers. Even without taking any of the Hugur sand yet, I swore I could feel happiness radiating from his soul and brushing against mine.

"Fucking fate, would you look at that," Rune murmured from behind me.

I turned toward him, smiling. "Me being able to touch him? I thought it was strange, too. Don't dragons burn anything they come into contact with?"

"No, they learned to control that." He searched my eyes. "But it's more than that, Frida. Eldi has bonded with you."

I drew back. "What?"

"Can't you feel it? The magic pulsing between you?" His smile widened, genuine happiness shining out of him. The sight of it left me dumbfounded, and for a moment, the world around us faded into the background. There was a twinkle in his eyes I'd never seen. Fate, he looked so handsome like this. So *alive*.

But then my mind registered his words, and a bolt of fear went through me.

"I can't have," I said, looking from Rune to the dragon and back again. "Only orcs can withstand dragon magic without it destroying them. I'm an elf. It'll turn me into a Draugr and drive me mad."

"I don't think so." Rune still smiled. "As I said, magic has changed these past few decades, and Eldi *chose* you. You didn't force him into this, like other folk did in the past. Besides, you're not the first. Lilia bonded with her dragon, and a dwarf named Astrid, who lives in the mountains, bonded with one, too. It hasn't turned either of them into a Draugr."

Heart pounding, I turned back toward Eldi. His crimson gaze bored into mine. And *yes*. There it was. Magic—delicious, beautiful magic—spun like weaving threads between us, dancing in the late-spring sunlight. I breathed it in, letting it fill me. But just as soon as it pressed against my soul, the dread came. If the guild knew I'd bonded with a dragon, they would use him in any way they could. They'd want him to kill their every enemy.

"Erik can never find out about this," I said roughly.

Rune's smile vanished. "No, he certainly can't."

"Don't speak of this back in the village. I doubt they'd purposely share it with anyone on the mainland, but you know how gossip spreads. We can't risk speaking a word about this to anyone."

"It's your news to share," he said, though his voice sounded strained, like he wasn't as happy about this as he'd been a moment before. And I didn't blame him. He didn't want the Hugur sand to end up in the wrong hands, and that was nowhere near as powerful as a dragon.

I took his hand in mine and held it against my heart. "You don't have to look so worried. I swear I won't let Erik find out."

"I know you won't, sunshine. I know you won't."

After that, Rune and I spread out a picnic to share with Eldi. We feasted on berries and a fresh loaf of bread slathered with butter. Rune had brought a bottle of wine, much to my surprise. We shared the whole thing. Even Eldi joined in, eagerly tipping back his head to drink. Laughter and stories passed between us. We didn't discuss the bond again, and I didn't dare bring up the guild. Not when the haze of happiness had settled over our little trio. I couldn't bear to chase it away with the dark cloud of our looming reality.

When the sun set, we climbed to our feet and

bid a goodnight to the dragon. We were no closer to solving his fear of flying than we had been before, but something felt as if it had shifted. Maybe it was the newly discovered bond or the realization that I had a real plan. But I felt hopeful for the first time since coming here—truly hopeful.

Everything would turn out all right. I'd return to the guild, where I'd be surrounded by my family. Erik would believe the magic had stopped me from reaching the island, and he'd give up his hunt for Rune. I'd find a way to get Eldi in the skies before I left. He'd have enough confidence to visit the village, where the kind townspeople would bestow lots of gifts and affection upon him. He'd never feel lonely again.

Nothing could stop me from making this happen. Except, perhaps, the ache in my heart when I thought about saying goodbye to Rune.

21

RUNE

I was fucked. Well and truly fucked.

Every time Frida smiled at me, it felt like my insides turned to liquid gold. Over the course of the past decade, I could probably count on one hand the number of times I'd made a joke, but I couldn't stop making them now. Her laughter was like the sun on my face after a long, hard winter. Until now, I'd been living in the dark.

But she was dead set on returning to the guild. And because of that, I could never let her know how I felt.

All I could do was hope she'd change her mind and realize she didn't belong with those people. They didn't deserve her smiles. Not that I thought she belonged with *me*, either—no one did—but she shone too brightly to spend the rest of her life surrounded by the worst kind of scum in the world.

Erik, especially. When I thought of her standing anywhere near him, I felt my hands tighten into fists.

I couldn't make that choice for her, though. She had to realize it herself.

And so when Freyasday came around again, I had the idea to suggest we head into the village for a day off from dragon-taming, woodworking, and archery. Frida had been avoiding me since our visit to Eldi's cave, and I'd accepted it without comment. But I also knew we didn't have long until Louisa's ship returned to collect Frida. If I wanted to show Frida how much she loved it here, I had to do it soon.

When I heard her rustling around in her room, I spread out a feast to break our fast. The day before, I'd spent hours trading in the village for a carton of eggs, some ham, a fresh loaf of bread, another wheel of Arvid's cheese, and an enormous bowl of berries. I set it out and waited. When Frida pulled open her bedroom door and saw me sitting there, she stopped short.

"Oh." Her cheeks turned red. "Good morning, Rune. I didn't expect to see you there. You're normally out the door before I am."

"Which is why I thought it'd be nice to share a

meal for once, when we're not so tired at the end of the day." I gestured at the elaborate spread.

"It does look delicious," she said uncertainly. "But Arvid will be waiting for me."

"Arvid knows I don't normally work on Freyasday."

"Is it Freyasday already?" she asked.

"They say time flies when you're working hard, eh?"

"I thought it was when you're having fun."

"Well, I suppose that means you're enjoying your time on the Floating Forest, eh?" Despite what felt like an encouraging smile from me, Frida still looked reserved. Had I done something to upset her? I wracked my brain, going over everything I'd said and done these past few days, but nothing stuck out to me. Her aloof attitude had begun that night we'd returned from the dragon cave, but I thought we'd had a nice time. We'd laughed and drank and shared stories far past sundown, until the fireflies had come to life to dance around our heads.

It had been one of the nicest evenings I'd had in a very long time. But Frida must not feel the same, and that knowledge twisted my stomach more than I thought it would.

She dumped her pack by the door, crossed the room, and eased into the chair opposite mine. Her eyes roved across the food. She went straight for the cheese. I couldn't help but smile.

"This is a different kind!" Frida exclaimed after tasting the cheese. The moan that spilled from her lips nearly made me come undone. Fate be damned, I wished my hands could conjure that sound. But she'd made it more than clear she didn't want me to touch her.

"That one is smoked," I said. "Thought you might like it."

"It's amazing, Rune. Thank you so much." She looked at me, and a watery sheen covered her eyes. But then she blinked it back so quickly I couldn't be sure if I'd imagined it. After that, we dug into the rest of our meal. With each bite, Frida let out a string of excited noises. Eventually, we'd indulged in most of the food, only leaving enough for Moira to enjoy an extra snack.

Frida let out a sigh of contentment, leaned back in her chair, and patted her belly. "You know, the guild meals are far less satisfying. It's basically gruel compared to all this."

"I know. I remember it very well," I said.

"Thank you for sharing it with me," she said. "In only a few days, this will all be lost to me for a very long time."

It doesn't have to be, I wanted to say. *Stay here,*

Frida. You'd be so much happier in this place with all the cheese and berries you could ever want.

But I knew what she'd say. She'd made her position clear, time and time again, and pushing her would lead nowhere. She had to encounter that moment herself—the life-changing, gut-churning moment when the world *shifted*, and you saw things in an entirely new light.

At least, I hoped she would.

"Speaking of enjoying things, I've planned for us to head into Oakwater this evening. I thought we could go watch the minstrels again." I cleared my throat, suddenly unsure if she'd accept after how uneasy she'd been around me lately. "It might be your last chance to dance, after all."

Her face clouded over. "You're right. The guild doesn't like dancing."

"Frida—" I started to say, then stopped myself. With a sigh, I stood and grabbed my plate to clear the table. I had to do something with my hands if I wanted to stop myself from saying something we'd both regret.

"Why do you think they do that?" she asked softly.

I paused, plate in hand. "The dancing ban?"

"All of it. The bad food, the celibacy, the rule to cut off anyone who isn't a member of the guild, even if they're your family. What is it all *for*, Rune?"

My heart pounded. This was the first time I'd heard her actually question things. I tried to quell my rising hope, but these were the very questions that had launched my own disillusionment. Pick at the seams, and it all unravels.

I put the plate back on the table and sat down, levelling my gaze on her.

"When you join the guild, you're no longer your own person. The guild is the body, and you're just a limb. You become the hand that holds the knife, or the fingers that reach into pockets to steal. If you have joy outside of that—a lover, a sister, a book that speaks to your soul—it reminds you of what life is like beyond your role as a tool. You remember you are your own person, which makes you yearn for a real life. And then it makes you leave." I gave her a grim nod. "The guild has so few members that it cannot afford to lose a single one. So they do what they can to control you and keep you from remembering the joys of life."

I'd probably said too much, but the words had poured out of me. Words I'd been dying to say to her since the start.

Frida blinked rapidly and clutched the edge of the table. After a moment, she stood and paced. I couldn't tell what she was thinking. Despite the shaking in her hands, her face was blank. She clearly didn't like what I'd said, but that could be for any number of reasons.

And so I let her pace. When I felt overwhelmed by emotion, the last thing I needed was for someone to ask me what I was thinking. She needed to work through her thoughts first.

Eventually, she came back to the table. Her eyes latched onto mine, and her lips parted, like she wanted to say something. But instead, she grabbed the remaining wedge of cheese and shoved it into her mouth.

When she'd finished chewing, she said, "Thank you, Rune. I would like to go see the minstrels tonight, like you suggested. But first, I'm going to visit Eldi."

And with that, she practically ran out the door, leaving me to wonder if I'd pushed her too far.

22

FRIDA

I spent the morning confessing everything to Eldi. The poor dragon had to listen to me go on and on about my feelings for Rune and my dread about returning to the mainland. Over the past few days, questions had been growing in my mind, questions I'd tried to bury under an avalanche of dirt. But they kept sprouting, stubbornly insisting I water them.

Why did the guild want to banish happiness?

How could my own father demand that from me?

Was Louisa right? Would I lose myself when I returned to the guild-hall and began carrying out my real assignments?

How would it feel when I left my newly bonded dragon behind? And Arvid? And…Rune.

I'd taken some Hugur sand to facilitate the conversation, just to ensure Eldi could understand me. When I'd finished laying out my questions, I felt a bit better for it. Nothing was solved, but acknowledging my problems out loud helped soften the sting of them.

Sighing, I sank onto the ground beside him and rested my forehead against his flank. The heat of him surrounded me like a hug.

My sweet friend, do you not see what you must do?

The voice rumbled through my mind, impossibly deep and gravelly. A jolt went through me, and I leapt to my feet. Heart pounding, I stared at Eldi, my lips parting. Had he...had he finally managed to speak to me? Or was I so distraught that I'd started hallucinating things now?

A rumbling went through my mind again. *It is me, sweet friend. You did not hear me speak before because you did not consume enough Hugur sand. This time, you did.*

I grinned, practically bouncing up and down on my toes. "I can't believe it, Eldi. I can hear your voice!"

Yes, and you should heed it. Do not go back to those people. They do not have your best interests at heart.

My smile plummeted. "But those people are my family."

Only a handful are. The rest are not. A pause. *You*

told me they left you to fend for yourself in the woods for years. You were just a child.

"Well, yes, because the guild has rules."

No rule would keep a good man from his daughter. If he truly cared for you, my sweet friend, he would have chosen you over a life of killing.

Eldi's words knifed through me. I sucked in a sharp breath, staggering away from him. Surely he couldn't mean that. Even though we were bonded, he didn't know my past and everything I'd gone through to get to this moment. If he did, he…

He might still say these very things.

Tears burning my eyes, I said, "From an outside perspective, I can see why you might think my father doesn't care for me, but my family has been a part of the guild for generations. It's who we are. It's in my blood. He was probably waiting for me to come to terms with it. He must have thought I'd come around eventually."

My sweet friend, look into your heart and ask yourself if you truly believe that. And before you make a decision you'll regret for the rest of your life, imagine what your future will be. Ignore what your ancestors did. What is it that you want, Frida? Choose your life for yourself.

I swallowed, taking a step back. Eldi's question was fair, but it made my stomach churn. I'd spent the past year with an all-consuming focus on one thing: joining my family. I hadn't allowed myself to question it or even contemplate a future that was anything else. It had been my way of coping with what I must do if I wanted to escape my loneliness.

Today's conversations with Rune and Eldi had formed cracks in the ground beneath my feet, and I didn't know where to step to avoid falling to a tragic fate.

"I need to go," I whispered. "I'll come back to see you tomorrow."

I look forward to it, my sweet friend. Ask Rune if he still has his dragon's saddle. I quite like the idea of trying out a short flight.

~

The village felt alive. It had been well over a week since I'd come into town, so focused was I on building Arvid's fence and learning how to communicate with my dragon. In just that short time, the streets had been transformed.

Already, the shell of Helga's new home took shape between the neighboring buildings. Strings of garland looped from one side of the road to the other, embellished with wildflowers, pine cones, and brown feathers. The minstrels had erected a wooden stage outside the tavern, where they were launching into an upbeat song for the villagers dancing nearby. Several folk, including Lilia, were weaving through the throng and handing out tankards topped with froth.

"What's all this?" I asked Rune. He stood tall beside me, clad in a snug-fitting cream tunic with twisting vines embroidered along the collar. He'd rolled his sleeves up to his elbows, which I found increasingly distracting. Something about the way his forearms flexed brought a flush of heat to my cheeks…and thighs.

Rune surveyed the boisterous street. "Since the Elding has moved on, the village is embracing the coming of summer. Everyone here prefers the outdoors and the open sky. Kind of like you, Frida."

I smiled up at him. "And you."

I still felt unsteadied by our discussion and my subsequent 'conversation' with Eldi. When I'd returned to the cottage, I'd expected Rune to pick up where we'd left off. I was sure he'd throw out more reasons why the guild wasn't my home. And while I didn't fully *disagree* with him, I also didn't want to talk about it right now.

He'd sensed my reluctance to talk, and I'd been relieved when he hadn't brought it up.

Now that we were here, I felt like I could breathe again. How could a girl feel trapped beneath a dark storm-cloud when minstrels were singing, pixies were dancing, and the best ale in the Isles was being passed around. As if reading my mind, Rune grabbed two tankards when Lilia bustled past.

"Here you are," Rune said reverently as he pressed the tankard into my hands. "Lilia's ale."

I took a timid sip. The smooth, rich liquid tasted of what I could only describe as magic. Surprisingly sweet, it vanished from my tankard far quicker than I'd intended. After I'd drained the entire thing, I caught Rune's laughing eyes as he watched me.

"Thought you might like that," he murmured.

A thrilling heat curled through me. "I'm surprised you're so fond of it. To me, it tastes like the kind of ale you'd find in a romance novel. It fits the descriptions I've read."

"Ah. That's because she's from around here. She probably modelled it off Lilia's ale."

I blinked. "I'm sorry, what?"

"Your favorite writer. She lives on the Isles. Last time I checked, she was in the Whispering Woods, over on the island called Hearthaven."

"I had no idea," I said, smiling. "I guess I just assumed she lived in a big city somewhere on the mainland."

I didn't know why it mattered, but the idea of Silva Sweetwater living in the Isles made a warmth flow through me. And to hear she might have based her stories on what she'd found here... Perhaps all those sweet moments, the perfect home, the friendships, and the romances really were possible, just like I'd always hoped.

The sound of music cut through my thoughts. On stage, the minstrels were thumping their feet against the wood and playing their instruments with gusto. Nearly the entire village had spilled out of their homes to fill the street. Helga and Valdar were spinning around each other, a wild light in both their eyes. It seemed the blanket picnic I'd set up for them had gone well, then. I beamed.

Suddenly, I was overcome with the need to let go of all my worries and ignore the path ahead, just one last time.

No matter what the future threw at me, I could have tonight.

I held out my hand. "Dance with me, Rune?"

"And risk me stepping on your feet?" he asked wryly.

"Don't make me beg," I said.

"I'd never make you beg, Frida." He took my hand and twirled me under his arm. With a surprising gracefulness, he pulled me against him, our bodies swaying in time with the beat. Our dance was not the frenetic jumping and leaping, like so many others, but I didn't dare complain.

Not when my heartbeat was a roar of thunder in my ears and my breath felt trapped in my lungs.

Rune leaned down and pressed his lips against my ear. When his breath caressed my skin, I shuddered. "I'm sorry it's not raining."

A full-body shiver went through me. "You remember me saying I like dancing in the rain?"

"Frida, I remember *everything* you've said."

I swallowed, Rune's steady warmth pulsing against me. When I tipped back my head to look up at his face, I found him already staring down at me. Something in my chest tightened. My mind raced. His words were what I'd always dreamed of hearing, but surely he didn't mean them the way I wanted. Surely the intensity of his gaze was only driven by…friendship?

I looked away, but Rune took my chin between his fingers and turned my head back toward him. His eyes were full of heat.

"Frida," he said. "I know I have no right to ask this, and dammit, I know I shouldn't. But I can't fucking help myself when it comes to you." His thumb caressed my jaw. "Some might say dragons are the most magnificent creatures alive, but they've got nothing on you. So before you leave my life forever, can I kiss you?"

My breath shuddered out of me. Inside my chest, my heart felt near to bursting, and his words repeated in my mind like a prayer. I tried to speak, but my voice felt trapped in my throat. So I answered him the only way I knew how. I gripped his tunic, pulled him down, and kissed him fiercely.

He groaned, his fingers tightening on my chin. His lips caressed mine, and a tumultuous need tore through me. Everything around us fell away. And as our bodies collided, it was as if time itself stood still. I poured everything into the kiss, pushing up onto my toes to get even nearer to him. He responded in kind, his free hand sliding around my waist and tugging me into his chest.

Too soon, the sound of clapping cut through the moment, bringing the world around us back into focus again. Sucking in a breath, I released my grip on Rune's shirt and tumbled back. A few folk had caught sight of our kiss and were clapping and cheering, like we'd just won at life. My cheeks flamed.

"All right, all right," Rune called out to the gawkers. "You've made your point. Move along now."

Our audience laughed, then drifted away, leaving me and Rune staring awkwardly at each other. My lips felt hot and swollen, even though our kiss had only lasted for a moment. It didn't feel nearly long enough. If anything, only briefly giving in to my feelings made them that much more potent, like flames were licking my skin.

"Sorry about that," Rune said, running a hand along the top of his head. "It's such a sleepy little village that it doesn't take much to get people excited."

Shyly, I asked, "Should we have another round of ale?"

He motioned toward Lilia, who'd just emerged from the tavern with a tray full of drinks. "After you."

We got another round. And then another. The sun soon vanished from the sky, giving way to a darkness that was speared through by an abundance of stars. After we settled onto a bench beneath the drooping leaves of a willow tree—Rune had built it years ago, of course—several of the villagers approached us and welcomed me to their island. I'd met a few last time, but only briefly. All were far more welcoming than they ought to be, given my secrets, and my uncertain guilt began to creep up as the night wore on.

There was a bone-crushing truth I was wrestling with. A life spent within the cold, sterile guild-hall, tasked to aim my bow at whoever I was commanded to target, no longer called to me the way it had before. In fact, I was quickly realizing it had never really called to me in the first place.

Deep down, I'd always known it, but I'd ignored that feeling. My family meant everything to me.

Except I hardly knew them.

They hadn't come for me when I'd run away. A year after I'd fled into the night, a note showed up on my front porch. They'd finally found me. But instead of asking me to come back home, all they did was wish me luck and tell me that my mother had passed away from her illness. It wasn't until years later that my brother came to pitch the idea of me joining the guild. Even then, my father kept his distance.

Rune shifted on the bench beside me, watching the minstrels pack up their things for the night. The street had emptied. Only Ragnar and Lilia remained. They carried empty tankards into the tavern, where hearth-light cast a luminous glow into the growing darkness.

"I suppose we ought to head back home," he said. "Are you all right? You've been quiet for the last half hour."

"Just taking it all in." Tipping back my head, I closed my eyes and breathed in the scent of the forest. "I love this place."

A moment stretched between us before he said, "Come on. There's something I want to show you."

The route to the cottage was shrouded in darkness, but Rune walked confidently, like he'd trodden this path a thousand times before. The forest was starting to feel familiar to me, too. So when we reached a fork, I expected us to turn left. Instead, Rune steered us to the right.

As we continued forward, the scent of brine curled through the trees, and I could hear the distant hiss of waves against sand. Soon the redwoods parted before us, and the moon's silver glow illuminated an endless stretch of sea that melted into the dark horizon. In unison, we came to a stop at the edge of the tree-line and gazed out at the expanse. The water stretched on for miles without even a dot of land marring the surface. It suddenly felt as if we were the only two people left in the world.

"It's beautiful at night," I whispered. "The sea, I mean." But really, I meant everything about this place: the forest, the village, the people. All of it called to my soul.

"So is this," Rune answered. I turned to find him leaning against the trunk of the nearest tree, holding a purple lily. Smiling, he held it toward me. "You said they were your favorites. Well, one of your many favorite things."

A sudden lump clogged my throat. "Rune."

"Frida."

"Why are you doing all these nice things for me?"

He pushed away from the tree and strode toward me, his muscular body backlit by the moon. "Because you shine brighter than the sun when you're happy, and you deserve to have everything that makes you feel that way. The flowers, the music, the dancing, the books, the cheese. Your new bonded dragon. All of it, Frida. You don't have to go back to that place. Everything you want is *here*."

My heart thundered in my ears.

"You forgot one thing," I whispered.

"Lilia's ale? Because you won't get that back in Erik's fucking cage, either."

"No, that's not what I meant," I said, trying to find the courage to voice it. "There's one more thing I want that's here. You."

Rune went very still, though his eyes swept back and forth across my face, as if he was searching for confirmation that what I'd said was true.

"Come on, Frida. Don't joke about that."

"Did that kiss feel like a joke to you?" I countered.

"No, it fucking didn't," he said in a low growl. Rune erased the distance between us, his eyes sparking with heat. "Does that mean you'll stay?"

I looked away, hating that I couldn't tell him what he wanted to hear—what we *both* wanted to hear. "How can I? If I stay here, Erik and my father will send someone looking for me. *And* you. I can't let that happen. Plus, the folk of Oakwater deserve peace, and we can't risk the guild discovering Eldi." I took a deep breath. "I've put a lot of thought into this, and there's only one solution to keep everyone safe. I have to return to the guild and tell them I wasn't able to step foot on the island. I can say the protective magic stopped me. Erik will have no choice but to give up on finding you."

Rune scowled. "What about the ship's captain that saw you come ashore?"

"Louisa didn't seem too fond of Erik. I think I can convince her to keep quiet about it. And if she seems resistant, I'll offer to steal some coin and pay for her silence."

"That's a terrible fucking plan," Rune said with a bitter laugh.

"It's the best plan I have!" I threw up my hands, tears blurring my vision. "Trust me, I have been falling apart trying to fix this impossible situation. And the only solution is to make myself miserable for the rest of my life!"

"I don't accept that," Rune shot back. "I'm going to make you happy, whether you like it or not."

"And I'm going to save your bloody life, whether *you* like it or not."

"Oh yeah? And what are you going to do if I toss you over my shoulder and lock you up in my cottage so that you can't throw yourself to the wolves?"

I narrowed my eyes. "You wouldn't."

"You underestimate my hatred for the guild and everything it stands for. If I had to choose between you hating me or you becoming one of them, you better fucking believe I'd choose to lock you up every damn time." His lips quirked up in the corners. "Fortunately, you've just given me a better idea."

Folding my arms, I glared at him. "Oh yeah? And what is that, Rune?"

"If you think the ship's captain will be willing to lie for you, then we make it a better fucking lie. We can say the magic not only stopped you, but it took your life. And if anyone tries to outsmart it again, the same thing will happen to them."

My stomach dropped. "Rune, no."

"Don't you see? As long as your captain friend agrees, it solves everything. You can stay here, where you're happy, and Erik won't send someone else." He shook his head, his eyes searching mine. "Give me one good reason we shouldn't do this."

"You're right. It would definitely stop Erik from sending someone else. But..." I blew out a breath, hating the tumultuous beating of my heart. "I can't bear the thought of my family believing I'm dead. And if I did this, I'd never see them again. Surely you can understand why that's not an easy decision for me to make."

Rune's eyes softened. "I know it isn't, Frida. Sleep on it, then. See how you feel in the morning."

23

FRIDA

Unfortunately, 'sleep on it' didn't work. Any hope of a restful slumber went out the window the second I climbed into bed and memories of Rune's kiss blazed in my mind like wildfire. I couldn't stop thinking about him. Or his 'solution' to all our problems. He'd come up with a decent idea, but could I really fake my own death?

Deep down, I knew I could if it weren't for my family.

How could they be a part of my life if I wasn't a member of the guild? And how could I *not* stay here, where I truly wanted to be?

Finding a solution felt impossible.

After a night of tossing and turning, I shuffled over to Arvid's house to complete the last section of his fence. He and his entire family were outside waiting for me, their arms bundled with an array of treats.

Beaming, Arvid bustled over to me with a wooden tray topped with well over a dozen different varieties of cheese. "For you, my lady."

I laughed, but I eagerly took the offered platter. "Arvid, what's all this? Our agreement was five wheels, and you already gave me three. There's... sixteen more here, if I'm counting correctly."

"Five didn't seem like nearly enough for how much work you've put into this." A wry grin spread across his bearded face. "Rune mentioned this is your very first woodworking job. Ever. I'm impressed by your work. Truly."

I felt myself brighten at that, like his praise and generosity was sloughing off some of my exhaustion. "Really?"

"Really." He nodded sagely. "It'll keep all our animals safe on the farm, and they can't wander off into the forest again. Plus, it's just in time for our two lost cows to return. Seemed they were having an adventure, but I'd rather not lose them again."

"Well, I'm glad it's all worked out, anyway." I smiled. "It's been an honor to build your fence, Arvid."

The rest of the family came over and handed me a basket of eggs, a mound of tea leaves, and a fresh loaf of bread. Shyly, Arvid's daughter came last with a quiver of arrows.

"Thank you for teaching me archery," Eydis said softly. "I wanted to give you this before you leave the island."

Ah. Suddenly, I understood why they were showering me with so many gifts. It wasn't just about my work on their fence. They thought I was leaving soon. And well, I probably was. I'd yet to decide whether I was rowing that boat out to Louisa's ship or not, but I'd yet to find another alternative. Rune's fake death plot didn't sit right with me.

"Thank you, Eydis. Did you make those yourself?" I asked her.

She nodded, her short ginger hair bouncing around her shoulders.

"You must have spent a lot of time on them. Tell you what, why don't you keep ahold of them for now and use them to practice? It'll make me awfully happy to know you're still working on your archery, even if I'm not here."

She brightened. "And when you come back, I can show you how much I've improved?"

I smiled, though my gut twisted. The likelihood of that happening was slim to none, but I couldn't bear to tell her that. Not when it might stop her from throwing her whole heart into something she loved.

"I'll look forward to it. I really will," I said.

"Thank you, Frida." Eydis threw her arms around my middle and hugged me tight. With tears in my eyes, I hugged her back and caught Arvid's smile across the way.

You should stay, he mouthed.

My glossy eyes transformed the dwarf into a blur of brown and orange.

If only I could.

Finishing the fence took longer than I'd anticipated. But when I finally hammered the final beam into place, the dwarves erupted into celebratory cheers against a backdrop of a sky painted orange. Fireflies were already buzzing about, filling the air with yellow raindrops. It was a beautiful sight to behold. I bid each of the dwarves a goodbye in turn, feeling heartsick because I knew this was probably the last time I'd see any of them.

The next morning, I emerged from the cottage at dawn to find Rune waiting for me outside his workshop with an axe strapped to his back and his old dragon saddle perched beside him. Crafted from rich leather and bolted together with forged steel, the contraption was nearly the size of me and must have weighed as much as a horse.

I pointed at the thing. "That wasn't what I was envisioning. It's at least five million times bigger than my horse's saddle. There's no way we're carrying that all the way to the cave. It's a good thing I've trained to ride bareback."

Rune chuckled. "Eldi's friendly, but he's no horse. If you want to ride him, you're going to need this. Trust me."

Nerves tingled in my belly. And suddenly, I wasn't quite sure my plan to *ride a dragon* was a particularly smart idea. I'd promised to get Eldi airborne, but he didn't need me strapped to his back for that. All he needed was a little encouragement. I could do that with my feet safely on the ground.

As if reading my thoughts, Rune knelt beside the saddle and pointed at some of the steel hooks. They were attached to leather strips. "These keep you locked into the saddle, so even if things go horribly wrong, you're not going to fall off the dragon."

"And if the dragon himself falls?" I asked, arching a brow.

"Dragons don't fall."

"Then why is Eldi so afraid of flying?"

Rune shrugged. "The same reason anyone is

afraid of anything, I suppose. His mind connects flying to something terrible that happened."

"Do you know what that is?"

"Afraid not. But seeing as he's chosen to bond with you, I'm sure you'll find out eventually."

I nodded, though I still couldn't shake the nerves. "All right. Let's get going, then."

"You know you can trust me, right?" he asked. "I wouldn't agree to help you with this if I thought there was any chance you'd get hurt."

I softened. "I do trust you, Rune. More than anything."

He looked like he wanted to say something, but then he shook his head and kept his mouth shut. Groaning, he hauled the massive saddle into his arms and grunted at me to take the lead. Our journey to the dragon cave took twice as long with the saddle. Every twenty minutes or so, Rune needed to stop and rest. Sweat covered his brow and coated his tunic, especially with the late-spring sun beaming down on us. I offered to carry it part of the way, but he refused to let me go near the thing. The only help he accepted was a few sips from my waterskin when we stopped.

Eventually, we reached the foothills, where we found Eldi prancing back and forth in the tall grass, like a cat who'd taken a long, deep sniff of catnip. When he spotted us dragging ourselves along the path, he raced toward us with his tail animatedly swishing behind him.

I laughed when he reached us and nudged my arm with his snout.

"I'm happy to see you, too. Sorry I couldn't make it yesterday. I got caught up finishing Arvid's fence."

When only silence answered me, I remembered the Hugur sand. I tossed a good dose into my mouth and washed it down with what was left of our water. Instantly, Eldi's voice filled my mind.

When you didn't come yesterday, I was worried you'd already left the island. I thought I'd never see you again.

With a sad smile, I rubbed his snout. "I'm not leaving until tomorrow night. That's when Louisa's ship returns."

Eldi sniffed the air. *You have the orc's scent on you. Is he your lover?*

I coughed at the sudden change in the conversation, my face flushing.

"Er, no. We just…" I glanced at Rune, who'd sat on the ground to catch his breath. He leaned against the saddle with his eyes closed. It didn't look like he was paying much attention to our conversation, but he was right there. He could hear every word I said out loud.

And so I tried to speak to Eldi through my mind, the same way he spoke to me.

We only shared a brief kiss. He's not my lover.

Eldi snorted in response. *I don't understand this 'brief kiss' business. Either he is your lover or he is not.*

Not. Very much not.

Then why is his scent all over you?

I really don't want to have this conversation with you. Can we focus on flying instead?

Hmm. Let him take some of the Hugur sand. I'd like to speak to the orc about his intentions with you.

"Absolutely not!" I exclaimed out loud.

"What's going on, Frida?" Rune asked tiredly.

"Nothing." My entire face flamed. "Eldi is just getting a little carried away, that's all."

Rune rose, scratching the base of his tusk. "Carried away about what?"

"Nothing. Absolutely nothing. I think we all just need to focus on why we've hauled that saddle halfway across the island."

"Now I understand why everyone found my dragon bond so irritating. You two were clearly having a full-blown conversation in your heads that you didn't want me to hear."

"Can we just move on, please?" I hissed at him.

He held up his hands. "All right, all right. Tell Eldi he needs to flatten his body against the ground so we can get the saddle fitted."

I sighed. "Eldi says he doesn't want you to speak through me."

"In that case, should I take some of the sand, too?" Rune asked.

"No!" I nearly shouted. "No, no. That's not necessary. You two don't need to talk." I shot a look at Eldi. *Please don't embarrass me.*

Eldi snorted again, but let it go. He lowered his belly to the ground and sprawled out like a beached whale, his breath rustling the grass. Rune hefted the saddle onto his glittering scaled back, then got to work cinching all the straps and hooks firmly into place. When he was finished, he stepped back and admired his handiwork with a distant look in his eye.

"It's about time someone got use out of this thing again," said Rune.

It's a shame it's just this once, I thought—more to myself than anything else.

If you will not stay for me, will you not stay for your lover?

He's not my lover.

I expected the dragon to argue some more, but he went silent as Rune helped haul me onto the saddle. It required a short climb using leather footholds that ran up the side of the saddle like a mini-ladder. When I reached the smooth seat, Rune gave me instructions to buckle myself in. Soon I was strapped into the saddle so tightly that I couldn't budge an inch.

Heart pounding, I gripped the horn that protruded from the leather. "Right. Are you ready for this, Eldi?"

His fear and excitement rushed over me. *I'm not certain I can do this. It has been twenty years since I last spread my wings.*

"That's all right," I said out loud. "All I want you to do is lift off the ground and hold flight for five seconds. Then you can land and catch your breath."

His scaly body trembled beneath me. *Five seconds.*

"Five seconds. I'll even count it down out loud." I leaned forward and rubbed his neck. "And remember, I'm right here with you."

A rush of trust and affection came toward me. Suddenly, the dragon rose and launched into a run. A wordless scream ripped from my throat, and I clung to the saddle's horn with every ounce of strength I possessed. I knew I wouldn't fall, not with the straps binding me to the saddle, but still I clung tight.

Fear rattled through me, but I managed to tamp it down enough for me to hide it from Eldi. And so, with the brilliant sun casting a haze of warmth upon the island, Eldi beat his wings against the humid air and lifted off the ground for the first time in decades.

The dragon soared.

"Five!" I shouted, hopefully loud enough for him to hear me. "Four! Three! Two! ONE!"

Eldi gently settled back onto the ground, his sharp talons slicing through the dirt. A heady exuberance came over him, filling my chest with the intensity of it. I found myself smiling so wide my cheeks ached, and I could hear Rune's excited shouts from behind us.

Leaning forward in the saddle, I brushed my hands along my dragon's scales. "Well done, Eldi. I'm so, so proud of you."

His happiness lit a fire in my soul.

Again? he asked eagerly.

"Absolutely," I said with a grin. "This time, how about we go for ten seconds?"

No, let's go for twenty.

24

FRIDA

"That was incredible!" I pranced from one end of Rune's cottage to the other, my heart so full I felt like I could stay awake all night. The morning's exhaustion felt years away, like it had belonged to someone else entirely.

Rune, however, eased into his chair beside the roaring hearth and closed his eyes, like he could fall asleep right then and there. "You, Frida Rurik, were crafted from pure sunshine and endless energy."

"Oh, come on," I said, sliding to a stop before him. "Don't pretend you didn't have fun today. I saw you smiling. And celebrating. And shouting, just like me."

His eyes cracked open. "You're right. It was one of the best days I've had in a very long time."

Heat curled through me. But as much as I yearned to climb onto his lap, I cleared my throat and turned away. "Thank you for helping me experience something so wonderful before I leave tomorrow."

Rune grunted. "And even that couldn't change your damn mind? You're willing to leave behind your bonded dragon and the joy of flying with him, and for what? To live a life you'll hate?"

"This isn't what I want, but I don't see another way," I whispered, my heart aching. I didn't want to spend our last night together like this, but I'd known it was coming. Neither of us could ignore the truth of what tomorrow would bring, no matter how much we wanted to.

"I gave you another way," he said in a low voice that shuddered over me. "Stay here. With Eldi. With Arvid, who I know you've grown fond of, too." A beat passed. "With me."

"Rune, you know I want to stay." Tears ran down my face now. I tried to wipe them away, but they just kept coming. "And if I could, I would. You have to believe that."

"What I believe is that you can't see the forest for the trees. You're so focused on the life you think you want that you can't see the life you could have, not even when it's right in front of you." With a frustrated sigh, he closed his eyes. "Good night, Frida. Sleep well."

I blinked, caught off guard by his sharp dismissal. Silently, I dabbed my face with my sleeve and walked away from him. This was not how I'd wanted to end things between us. But anything more would be unfair to him. Rune had already given me so much. I couldn't ask for more. I couldn't ask for him to wrap his arms around me and give me one last memory of what life was like beyond the guild.

One last moment of joy.

Something I could hold on to when the guild-hall felt too small and too dark.

Something to remind me of why I'd gone back —to save him and everyone else here.

I went into my room without a word. As soon as the door was shut, I slumped against it and sank to the floor. I dropped my head into my hands and mourned a future that could have been. Me and Rune, waking up beside each other every morning. Hazy days spent building and training archery and soaring through the skies on the back of the dragon, who I realized I'd already come to love. Nights in front of the hearth with Moira curled up at our feet.

In my mind, it was a lovely little life. One I could never claim as mine.

The weight of the door suddenly vanished from behind me. I fell back, my head colliding with a pair of worn leather boots. I looked up into the oak moss face of the orc who'd shown me the kind of life I could have had, if only I hadn't been born into the wrong kind of family. Maybe in another life, we could find each other again, and we wouldn't have the long blade of the guild hanging over us.

Rune swept me up into his arms and carried me into the main room. He gently lowered me into the rocking chair, his eyes searching mine. Everything within me tensed.

"I'm so sorry, Frida," he murmured, kneeling before me. "I don't want to argue with you, especially not on your last night here. That's not how I want us to spend our last few hours together."

Something in my chest stirred, that aching sense of loss I'd felt earlier with Eldi. Rune's eyes, so rich and brown and kind…they felt like home.

"I don't want that, either," I said.

He smiled. "Good. What would you like to do, then?"

Kiss you. Hold you. Touch you. I want to love you, Rune.

Rune's eyes went wide, and a shudder went through him. Gone was his smile. In its place was the look of a man starved. He cupped my cheek, his thumb on my jaw and his fingers spread across my neck. An unrelenting need tore through me, my eyes locking on the closeness of his lips, his tusks.

"Eldi convinced me to take some of the Hugur sand during one of your flying breaks," he murmured. "He poked a talon at the sack very insistently. I thought he wanted me to take it so I could hear his thoughts in case you two got into trouble when you were up in the air. Then he started badgering me with questions."

The roaring of my thundering heart filled my ears. "Wait, what are you saying?"

I heard your thoughts just now.

The implications shuddered through me, burning my cheeks. He'd heard my thoughts about wanting him. I started to pull back, to put some space between us before he could do it himself. With the fear of tomorrow looming before me, I couldn't bear the weight of his rejection, too.

But then his voice filled my mind again. *I want all those things, too. Why do you think I'm fighting so hard for you to stay? It's because I've fallen for you, Frida. In the few weeks you've been here, you've become the best part of my life. I'd do anything not to lose you.*

"Oh, Rune," I whispered. My tormented heart lifted in my chest. The idea that we'd found our way to each other like this—a would-be assassin and her prey—seemed laughable. But it also felt like the most inevitable thing in the world. The moment I'd laid eyes on Rune, my world had been forever changed.

Rune braced his palms on the arms of the chair, boxing me in place. Even though he was on his knees, our faces were level, and so when he leaned in, his mouth captured mine. My soul sighed, even as an unrelenting fire blazed through me. I gripped the front of his tunic, relishing the soft warmth of his lips and the cooling touch of his tusks that gently pressed against my skin.

After a moment, Rune pulled back. The need in his eyes burned hot. Excitement pounded in my ears, my heart racing so fast I could barely breathe. Desire tightened between my thighs. I slid my hand around his broad neck as he leaned back in, his lips trailing down my chin. Every touch sparked a new flame, intensifying the growing ache in my core.

A satisfied rumble sounded in his throat, and his hand swept down the front of me to cup my breast. A gasp popped from my parted lips, and my thighs trembled.

Fate, I wanted him. Inside me, on top of me, under me, against the wall. I wanted him everywhere and anywhere. For hours. For days.

For *months.*

He chuckled softly, his breath hot against my

neck. "I'm more than happy to oblige, but I'm hoping we can take some breaks for sleep every now and again."

"Don't forget food," I said with a smile.

"Maybe I can eat it off you," he murmured against me.

A thrill went through my core. Rune gently squeezed my breast, as if sensing my response to his words, then brushed his thumb across my peaked nipple. Even over the top of my tunic, his touch made me gasp.

"Fucking fate, I love that noise, Frida," Rune said, pulling back. "I'm on my knees before you, willing to do whatever you want. Tell me what you like."

"I like *you*," I whispered, my heart pounding.

"Hmmm. You can do better than that." His eyes darkened as his free hand slid around to the top of my thigh. He slipped his thumb between my legs, pressing it firmly against my core. An aching need pulsed through me. "Do you want my finger here, or my tongue?"

I swallowed. The idea of his mouth against me brought a pool of wetness to my thighs. Rune's eyes sparked, and that hungry look consumed his face once more. Everything I was feeling, he felt, too. It was as if the Hugur sand had bonded us in a way I'd never imagined.

"Tongue it is." He grinned, pressing his thumb harder against me. I wriggled against him, desperate to erase the distance between us. I needed more. So much more.

"What about your tusks?" I gasped.

"Oh, don't you worry about them, sunshine. I know how to use them to make you squirm."

Oh my.

His hand moved to my trousers. He unlaced them and slid them down my legs, then pulled back to drink in the sight of me. My entire body trembled at the curl of his lips and the wicked satisfaction glinting in his eyes.

Still on his knees, Rune lowered his head. He brushed his lips against my knee, and a shudder went through me. Smiling against me, he slowly skated his left tusk up the side of my leg and stopped only an inch short of brushing my core. I cried out as an aching need blazed through me.

I slid my fingers into his thick, dark hair and tugged his mouth toward me.

"Please," I gasped. "I want you to taste me."

"I'll do anything you want, sunshine," he said. His cool tusk skated across my wetness, driving me mad.

When his mouth finally found me, I nearly came undone. Pleasure shuddered through me, sparking stars in my eyes. I arched against the chair, my hands still twisted in his hair. And as Rune's tongue swept across me, my pleasure already began to mount.

It had been so long since anyone had touched me, and even then, it had never felt like this. Like he knew exactly where to caress me and what I liked. Like he could spend all day on his knees if that was what I needed.

His tongue dove inside me, then slid up to my clit. And then I broke. Crying out, I gripped the chair, quakes of pleasure rocking through me. Rune kept his tongue pressed tightly against my core until my orgasm slowed. Soon I was nothing more than a trembling mess against him.

Rune pulled back and looked up at me. I smiled and curled my fingers across the side of his face, feeling more content than I'd felt in a very long time. But then he smirked, and that heat between my thighs returned.

Rune stood, tugged me off the chair, and gently lowered me onto the rug spread before the hearth-fire. The flames cast flickering light onto his face as he settled his powerful body on top of mine. He caught my mouth in his and kissed me with a hunger that stole all the breath from my lungs.

Between kisses, Rune pulled off my shirt, then followed it with his own. Heart in my throat, I spread my fingers across his chest, feeling the softness of his skin and every dip and rise of his hard-won muscles.

"You're beautiful," he murmured, gazing down at me.

"So are you," I whispered back.

With his eyes locked on mine, Rune slid his body between my thighs, and his hard length pressed against me. I gasped at his size. Just like everything else about him, he was large enough to make my pulse race.

Are you sure you want this? I heard him ask.

I've never been more sure of anything in my life.

And as I gazed up at him, I felt something pass between us that I'd always dreamed of finding. Happiness. Contentment. Hope. Against all odds, I'd found the thing I'd been looking for all my life.

I'd fallen in love with Rune.

I've fallen for you, too, Frida. In every possible way.

Tears filled my eyes. I couldn't leave him. Not for my brother. Not for my father. And certainly not for the fucking guild. Suddenly, it felt as if a film had lifted from my eyes, and I could see the world for how it truly was. As much as I loved my family, I couldn't lose who I was just to have them in my life. I needed to live for myself.

I needed to choose my own happiness.

Rune searched my gaze, the Hugur sand allowing him to read my every thought.

"Does this mean what I think it means?" he asked, almost timidly.

"Yes, Rune," I said, the tears sliding down my face now. "I want to stay here. I want to start a life on this island, one with you by my side. If you'll still have me. But I can't promise it'll be easy."

"I would have you, even if the storms plagued my every step. I don't care if it's hard. You're worth it, Frida. You're worth everything."

With his hand cupping my waist, he slid inside me. I gasped at the feel of him and how well his hard length filled my core. He slowly inched inside until he hit the very back of me. Another shudder shook my body.

"Fucking fate," Rune said, groaning. "You feel so fucking good. I don't think I can control myself."

I met his eyes. They were only an inch from mine. Everything within me soared.

"Then don't," I whispered.

Rune gripped me tighter. He pulled back, then thrust deep inside me. I gasped, arching against him. Bracing his arms on either side of my head, he thrust again, harder and faster than the time before.

But it wasn't enough. I wanted more.

As his pace quickened, I curled my fingers around the rug and hooked my legs around his hips, a desperate need coming over me. His cock hit the back of me again, filling me completely.

Rune's lips found my ear, but it wasn't his voice I heard.

I love you, Frida.

My pleasure stormed forward.

I love you, too, I thought back.

And then I reached the edge, my orgasm pounding through me once more. Rune's pleasure reached its crescendo a second later, as if my moans fuelled his. Together, we breathed, holding tight to each other, sweat coating our skin. It was a long time before either of us moved, and when we did, we didn't dare let go.

25

RUNE

Sunlight slanted through the open window, casting luminous light on Frida's bare back. Smiling, I drew lazy circles across her skin and buried my face in her hair, breathing in the floral scent of her. Fate, I couldn't remember the last time I'd felt this much at peace.

I didn't know if I ever had.

Sleepily, she nestled against me, curled up with one thigh tossed over mine and her head on my chest. Her breath tickled my skin, but I didn't dare move. Right now, I wanted nothing to shatter this perfect moment. I just kept reliving the memory of her telling me she wanted to stay.

I wasn't naive. People often said things they didn't mean in the heat of the moment. It wasn't that I thought she'd lied to me. At the time, I'd felt how deeply she believed it. But in the dawn of a new day, would she feel the same? The Hugur sand had long since worn off, so I no longer had that link to her emotions. She could be thinking anything.

"Good morning," I eventually said, kissing the top of her head. "Did you sleep okay?"

"Hmm." Giggling, she tipped back her head to gaze up at me. "Not particularly. Someone kept poking me with something."

It was true. After we'd made love by the hearth, I'd carried her into the bedroom, where we'd explored each other again. And then we'd both drifted off to sleep—until a few hours later when I'd awoken to find her naked body pressed against mine. That was all it took to rouse me from slumber. It seemed I couldn't get enough of her.

"I'd apologize, but it didn't sound like you minded," I said.

"I didn't mind at all." Her voice went soft. "In fact, I wouldn't mind if every day ended exactly like that."

I tensed. Here it was. She'd tell me she wished it could be like this, but that, of course, it couldn't. Tonight, she'd board Louisa's ship and return to the mainland. As soon as she docked, Erik would get his claws into her. And I'd never see her again.

Fucking fate.

Clearing my throat, I said, "You don't need to

explain yourself. I'm glad we had last night together, even though that's all it was."

Frida pushed up onto her elbow and frowned down at me, her chestnut hair sliding into her face. "What are you talking about?"

"I know you need to leave," I said evenly. "Last night, we both got carried away—"

"*Carried away?*" Brow furrowing, Frida rolled off my chest, snatched the blanket, and covered herself. Then she stood and backed away, shaking her head. "Was that all it was to you? Getting carried away?"

"No, it wasn't. Not for me." I threw my legs over the side of the bed and stood. This wasn't a conversation to have lying down.

"Then I don't understand what you're saying. I told you I wanted to stay, and I thought you knew I meant it. I thought you could *feel* that I meant it." She pressed a shaking hand to her heart.

"But I know how badly you've wanted to get back home," I said softly. "I won't hold you to something you said in the heat of the moment."

"I'm in love with you, Rune," she whispered. "I don't want to live my life without you."

"I don't want that, either. Fuck, I'm so in love with you that I'd sail you back to the mainland myself if that's what would make you happy."

"Well, that's not what I want!" she exclaimed.

"Then get the fuck back over here."

She dropped the blanket, rushed toward me, and launched into my arms. With a satisfied grunt, I tossed her onto the bed. Bracing my arms on the pillows, I leaned in and kissed her, showing her just how much I'd meant what I'd said. Eventually, she hooked her leg around my hips and started squirming. I went rock hard.

"We need to talk about tonight," I murmured against her lips.

She sighed. "Right now? Maybe we just ignore Louisa's ship. She'll go away and come back later."

I pulled back. "I don't think postponing the inevitable is a good idea."

"You're probably right."

"So what do you want to do? It's your call."

"We don't have many options, do we? I'll have to ask Louisa to lie about what happened to me." The sadness in her eyes sliced through my heart like a knife.

"There might be another way…" I said.

"Do you have one?"

"No," I said, shaking my head. "I've thought a lot about it, and I can't see another solution."

"Neither can I." She slid her soft fingers up the side of my neck, then tugged me toward her. "We know what we have to do, and I don't want to talk about it anymore. Kiss me?"

I gazed down at her, wishing there was something more I could do. In my gut, I truly believed she'd be happy here—far happier than she'd ever be back in the guild. That place and those people would make her miserable. Eventually, she'd become a husk of the elf I'd come to love. But I also knew she hated vanishing on her family like this. They might not have done right by her, but she clearly loved them and would mourn their absence in her life.

"Don't make me beg, Rune," she whispered.

"Never," I promised.

26

FRIDA

Heavy clouds blotted out the moon, drowning the shoreline in an impenetrable darkness. The waves lapped at our boots. In the tense silence, the sound of the sea seemed as loud as a dragon's roar. Rune stood resolutely beside me with a steadying hand on my back. Before we'd left, I'd told him I understood if he needed to stay at home. Encountering an ice giant, even though it had been decades since Isveig's fall, might not be a particularly pleasant experience for him, but he'd insisted on accompanying me to the ship. If something went wrong, he wanted to be there.

I waited with my chin held high, but nerves tumbled around my belly. This was the right decision for me—that much was certain. But it didn't come without an aching sense of loss. I'd never again see my family, my home, my old neighbors, or my horse. As much as I would choose this life, over and over again, I wished some things could be different.

I knew I'd likely never stop missing my family.

An orange light flashed in the distance, and Rune's hand tightened against my back. Louisa's signal. She was here. If I flashed a light back or never showed, she'd move on and return in another two weeks. And that would be her final attempt to retrieve me.

"Are you ready?" Rune asked.

"No, not really. There's a chance she could laugh in my face."

"It's still not too late to change your mind," he said. "We can turn around now, return to the cottage, and spend the next two weeks ignoring the world."

"No, you were right before. I don't want to put it off and have it hanging over my head any longer."

He nodded. "After you, then."

I grabbed the edge of the boat and tugged it into the water. Rune followed after me, climbing inside. He took the back, while I took the front, and together we rowed toward the distant ship. Every now and then, Louisa's signal flashed in the darkness, helping lead the way. It was a good hour or so before the tiny rowboat slid through the dark waters near the ship.

From the deck, a shout rang out. Soon a rope ladder dropped over the side, and Rune and I anchored our boat to climb.

When we reached the railing, Louisa was waiting for us with her hawk perched on her shoulder. Several other ice giants fanned out behind her, armed with swords. A tense hush fell across the ship.

Louisa eyed Rune, but she spoke to me. "Frida, I'm glad to see you're still in one piece, but I must say I'm surprised to see an orc on board my ship. Care to explain?"

"It's a long story. To share in private. Will you tell your men to stand down?"

She flicked her eyes my way, then instantly swung them back to Rune. "I'm sure you can see why I might not think that's a smart idea."

"I mean you no harm," Rune said with his hands raised.

"Last time I checked, orcs hated us ice giants," Louisa said, narrowing her eyes. "And for good reason."

"Were you involved in Isveig's invasion?" Rune asked.

Louisa scowled. "Absolutely not."

"Then I hold no ill feelings toward you."

"Hmm." Eyes still narrowed, she held up her hand to motion at her crew. "Stay back. I'm taking Frida and the orc into my cabin for a private chat. I want three of you to stand guard outside. If you hear shouting, feel free to barge in."

When I opened my mouth to argue, Louisa shot me a murderous look. "You should be happy I'm giving you this much. If you were almost anyone else, they would have cut you down already."

"All right. Sit down." Louisa motioned at two high-backed leather chairs that perched on one side of her cluttered desk. She stood on the other side, pouring whisky into three dented tin cups that had seen better days. As I took a seat, she slid one across the table to me, the next to Rune, and then she downed the third herself in a single gulp.

She poured herself another and plopped into her chair. Instantly, her hawk settled onto the desk beside her and eagerly took an offered bit of bread. Maps curled on the wall behind her, where the humidity had soaked into the parchment. The dim light of her oil lamp cast shadows onto her pale blue face.

"Time to explain what the fuck is going on," she said.

"The guild lied to me," I said, lacing my hands in my lap.

Frowning, Louisa propped her legs on the desk, crossing them at the ankle. "I'm going to need a bit more information than that."

"All right. As you guessed, this was my first assignment." I tossed the original parchment onto the desk, and her hawk poked his beak at it. "That's the task I was given."

She arched a skeptical brow. "Am I allowed to read that?"

"By guild rules? No."

Louisa chuckled. "You're playing with fire, Frida."

I shrugged and waited. The cabin was tense and silent, save for the creaking of the ship as it swayed. Eventually, Louisa snatched up the note, unfolded the parchment, and read every word. By the time she'd finished with it, the confusion on her face matched my initial feelings.

"They wanted you to steal a fucking dragon?" She dropped the parchment, like it might bite her. Then she pointed at the stoic orc who sat silently beside me. "Let me guess. That's Rune."

"The very one," he answered.

"Do you have a dragon?" she asked frankly.

"No, he doesn't. That's not the real reason Erik sent me here," I said, leaning forward. "He wanted me to...well, what he really wanted was—"

"Let me guess. Erik knows about the magic that protects the islands, so he lied to you about your assignment. Since then, he's been in contact to tell you what he really wants you to do. Which is to assassinate the orc, I'm guessing."

"Well, yes," I said, surprised she'd pieced it together so quickly.

"Don't look so shocked," she said with a small smile. "I'd already wondered if he found a loophole. I thought it might be something like this, but I didn't dare ask. He doesn't like people asking questions."

"He doesn't like a lot of things," I said.

"Yeah, and I'll tell you one thing I know he doesn't like. His guild members not completing their assignments." She jerked her thumb at Rune. "Why's he still alive? And better yet, why are we talking about this in front of him?"

I pursed my lips, hating the traitorous heat that filled my cheeks. "Well."

Louisa's eyes went wide. She pointed at Rune, then pointed at me, then shook her head and laughed. "Oh, I think I have a pretty good idea what's happened here."

"Do you remember what you told me just before I got into the rowboat?" I asked.

"I said you're not like the others. Looks like I was right."

"Very right. The truth is, I only wanted to join the guild for my family. They've always been a part of it. So I thought I needed to be a part of it, too." I shook my head. "But I was wrong."

She folded her arms, leaning back in her chair to eye the two of us. "Listen, I'm sympathetic to your story. I really am. And I would *love* to help you. But if I try to smuggle you back in without Erik knowing, we'll all get caught. He'll have someone waiting at the docks for us."

I exchanged a quick glance with Rune. His steady nod grounded me.

"I don't want you to smuggle us back in," I said. "I'm staying here on the island with Rune."

She cocked her head, surprised. "Oh, in that case, congratulations. I'm happy for you, I really am. You deserve better than what the guild can give you." She reached for the whisky. "Let's toast to it."

"Before you get too excited, I do need your help."

Her smile dimmed. "I'm scared to ask."

We were so close. I could feel it. Louisa clearly thought little of the guild, and I felt encouraged by her happiness at hearing I wanted to stay. All I needed was to provide some assurances that Erik would never find out—that she wouldn't be at risk if she helped me. And I had to trust she was the person I hoped she was.

Swallowing, I nodded at Rune. He unhooked the burlap pouch attached to his belt and dropped it on the desk. We'd used most of it, but there was enough left for Louisa to communicate with her beloved hawk a few times. It seemed like something she'd like.

Louisa pinned her gaze on the pouch. "Is that some sand?"

Instead of answering, I said, "I want you to tell Erik I died trying to cross the magical barrier that protects the island. In exchange, you can have that. Our only request is that you be careful with it. And never tell anyone else what it is."

She sniffed the air. "What kind is it, then? With the way you're acting, I'd think it was Fildur, but it doesn't smell like fire."

"It's called Hugur sand," Rune said, his gaze turning dark. "And I'll only tell you what it does if you agree to our requests."

Louisa laughed, poking the pouch. "You know, if I hadn't spent a couple weeks with Frida on my ship, I'd think you two were trying to scam me. I didn't get to where I am today by being a fool."

"You can look at it if you want," I said.

For a moment, Louisa didn't make a move for the pouch. Long moments of silence stretched between us, putting pressure on the hope in my chest. I wanted to believe she'd come around, but it had always been a long shot. Anyone who knew anything about the guild would never dream of double-crossing them, especially not for some unnamed sand.

But eventually, she sighed and pried open the pouch. She took a closer sniff.

"All right. You're not lying about it being magic, but it doesn't smell like any of the four elements. What is this stuff?" She looked from me to Rune.

"I'll tell you if you agree to our requests," he said, steepling his hands beneath his chin.

Louisa cracked a smile. "I can see why you like him, Frida." She tapped her chin. "If I tell Erik you're dead, you can never again step foot on the mainland. He can never find out I lied..." She winced, dragging her nail across her throat. "And while I'm willing to lie for you, I'm not willing to die."

Pain lanced through my heart. Taking a deep breath, I ignored it, reached across the table, and took her hand in mine. "The last thing I want is for anyone to get hurt. That's partly why I'm doing this. I hope it'll stop Erik from sending someone else to the Isles."

She patted our joined hands. "It's a good idea. But what about your family?"

I looked away. "It was wrong of them to ask me to become something I'm not. And as much as I hate that they'll never know the truth about what happened to me, there's no other way."

"Well, all right, then. I guess we've got a deal," Louisa said, her eyes snapping down to the pouch. "Now tell me what's in there."

I let Rune take over from there. While he explained the Hugur sand's magic to Louisa, I stood and trailed across the room to peer out the porthole. A breeze blew across the sky, sweeping away the dark clouds that had plagued the night. Silvery light now illuminated the rippling water and the tiny island in the distance.

Convincing Louisa had been easier than I'd expected, and soon Rune and I could board our little boat and return home. A bright future lay before me, the kind I'd always wanted. But beneath the hope, the victory felt almost hollow, which was ridiculous.

I supposed that was just how life was. You won some things and lost so many others. In time, I knew the pain would fade. I would never forget the family I'd once had, but I could build a new one, full of people who loved me for who I was instead of people who wanted me to be someone else entirely.

So when Louisa stood and shook hands with Rune, I let the joy fill my heart. Everything was going to be just fine. Together, we'd solved the impossible.

27

FRIDA

The next morning, I awoke in Rune's arms, safely tucked into the crook of his shoulder. We'd spent all night 'celebrating' the true start of our new life together, and while I'd hardly slept, I felt as fresh as a purple lily. Smiling, I unwound myself from his embrace and padded out of the bedroom to get ready for the day.

"I love you, Frida," he said sleepily when I reached the door.

I paused and cast a smile over my shoulder at him. "I love you, too."

The next few weeks passed in a haze of happiness and hard work. Now that Arvid's fence was done, I joined Rune on his builds. With the help of the villagers, we finished up Helga's house and moved on to Lilia's new place. On some afternoons,

I trained Eydis. On others, I made the trek to Eldi's cave, where we practiced flying. With every day, he grew bolder and flew further.

And after two full weeks of shorter trips, we made it all the way to Oakwater. When we landed on the outskirts of town, a crowd awaited us. Arvid and his entire family had come out for support, along with Lilia, Ragnar, Helga, and Valdar. They clapped and cheered, throwing their fisted hands in the air with an exuberance that reminded me all too well of my brother back home.

I still missed him terribly, and as I swung off my dragon's back, a pang went through my heart. Deep down, I knew it hadn't been long, and it would take time for the pain to heal. It didn't mean it hurt any less than it did right now, though.

Rune crossed the distance between us and swept me up into his arms, spinning me around in a slow circle. When he stopped and drew back to look at me, he beamed. "I knew you could do it, you brilliant ray of sunshine."

"It was all Eldi. I was just there to help him remember what he could do," I said.

Rune cocked his head. "What's wrong, my love?"

"Nothing's wrong."

But Rune didn't look like he believed me. Even without the Hugur sand, it often felt like he could read my emotions. And as much as I loved that he could understand me in a way that no one else could, I didn't want him to dwell on my sadness. The last thing I wanted was for him to believe I regretted my decision to stay here.

Gently, he lowered me to the ground and started to say, "Is this about—"

But Helga sprang over to us before he could finish his thought. "Congratulations, Frida! I know you've been working with the poor beast for weeks, and look at him now!"

I smiled. "He's done so well. I'm proud of him."

"Well, listen. You know how we've been talking about getting the Dragon Festival up and running again?"

"Right." I nodded. "Lilia mentioned it to me. She said you all were trying to sort it out for real this time."

"I must admit, I already have." She grinned at me sheepishly. "We want to throw it on Freyasday of this week, to celebrate Eldi's first successful flight to Oakwater. But since he's your dragon and a wee bit shy, I wanted to tell you before we got it all set up."

"Oh!" I looked up at Rune, who wore a bemused expression. "Did you know about this?"

"No, they kept this quiet from me, too," he said with a low chuckle.

"So." Helga grasped my hands in hers. "What do you say?"

At the edge of the group, Eldi shifted. I gazed over at him, arching my brow in question. Now that we'd traded away the last of our Hugur sand, I could no longer hear his voice in my head, but we'd learned to communicate in other ways. Deep down, I expected him to rebuke this offer. Helga was right. Unlike Lilia's dragon, Eldi wasn't particularly fond of attention.

But slowly, he lowered his head, confirming his agreement to the festival.

With a grin, I turned back to Helga. "Well, it looks like you're going to get your party. Eldi is happy for you to do it."

"Oh, this is incredible!" Bouncing on her toes, Helga clapped and hopped away to inform the others. Rune slid his arm around my shoulder, pulling me in close. The warmth of him radiated through me.

"I don't know what she would have done if you'd said no," he said with a low chuckle.

I shook my head, watching her share the news with everyone else. "She might have knocked her house down again, just to make us rebuild it for her as a punishment."

Rune laughed, a deep, throaty sound that warmed every inch of me, soothing away my earlier sadness. I nestled against him, relishing his love and the cheerful chatter of my new friends. Life did not have to be perfect to be good.

Shouts erupted from down the road. The bubbling conversation ceased as we all turned toward the noise. The shadow demon minstrel rushed down the road. His eyes were wide, fear painting his every feature.

Instantly, Rune went tense and took control of the situation. He pulled away from me, reaching the shadow demon in two quick strides. "What's happening?"

"Some folk just came ashore," he said quickly, rubbing his hands together in great agitation. "They asked where they could find you." His eyes darted to me. "They said they're Frida's family. And that they're from the Assassin's Guild."

28

FRIDA

I nearly fell to my knees, and the gasp that scraped its way from my throat left me breathless. Horror writhed in my stomach like a mass of snakes. All I could think was that I'd doomed them all. The guild had come here looking for me. *No wait, that's not right.* They thought I was dead, so they must have come looking for Rune. Did they think he'd had something to do with it?

"Hey, love." Helga was by my side in an instant. Gently, she took my arm and held me still. I realized I was shaking.

I shook my head wordlessly.

"Everything's going to be all right," she said with a calm certainty that defied logic. How could everything be all right?

"I'm so sorry," I whispered to her. "I've brought this on all of you."

"Don't be silly." She tightened her hold on my arm. "You're one of us now, and we're right here beside you, no matter what happens next. You hear me?"

I didn't deserve her loyalty, but I nodded all the same. That was when I noticed all the other gathered villagers had wandered over, standing in a line by my side. Arvid nodded at me. So did Mellor and Lilia. They were all here. I felt bolstered by their support.

Rune exchanged a few quiet words with the minstrel, then came to stand beside me, too.

"What's going on?" I asked. "Did Erik come?"

"You're about to see," he said quietly.

As if on cue, two figures appeared in the distance, striding purposefully down the center of the village road. I sucked in a sharp breath. The taller figure wore mottled gray leathers that amplified his powerful frame, and his chestnut hair hung loose around his broad shoulders. Beside him, the shorter figure was a near copy. The only difference was, he wore black leathers and had my slighter frame.

It was *them*. A piece of me I'd never been able to forget.

Tears filled my eyes, and I took off toward

them, my boots pounding the dirt road. Rune called out after me, but I couldn't stop now. Not when my father and brother were *here*, against all odds.

I knew the moment Logi spotted me. His eyes caught mine, and every muscle in his body tensed. Abruptly, he stopped. My father saw me a second later. He, too, slowed to a halt in the middle of the road. His hands fisted beside him.

At the horror-stricken looks on both their faces, I stopped running. They gazed at me across the village, and when I tried to find my voice, it abandoned me.

Eventually, my father cleared his throat, his expression still full of torment. "So it's true."

"What?" I didn't understand. *What* was true?

"You look good, Fri," my brother choked out. "You wear life in the wilderness well. You always have."

I looked from my father to my brother and back again, confusion roiling through me. "What's going on? How are you here? Didn't you think..."

The sadness in my father's eyes deepened. "Didn't we believe you were dead? That's what you wanted, wasn't it? For us to think we'd shipped you off to your end."

A sharp pain lanced through me. "No, that's not what I wanted."

"You had the ship's captain tell us just that," he said.

Shame rushed through me, but it was muted by a sudden burst of anger. "What else could I have done? If you knew I'd stayed by choice, you would have…well, you would have shown up here, just like this! And *you* would have no hesitation to—" I stopped myself before I mentioned Rune, and I refused to let myself look over my shoulder at him. They might not have noticed him yet.

"We didn't come here to kill the orc, Fri," my brother said, holding up his hands to show he had no weapons. No swords, no daggers, nothing. "If we did, we wouldn't be standing on this island right now. The magic would have stopped us from coming ashore."

That much was true. So then why were they here?

"We came here for you," my father said. "After Louisa told Erik your story, she saw how torn apart I was and later came to me privately. She wanted me to know the truth about what happened to you." He shook his head. "I didn't know Erik's true reasons for sending you to the island. I had my suspicions, of course. But I didn't know who Rune was or his history with the guild. Well, I did, but he went by another name back then."

"Wait, what?" I whispered, my heart pounding.

Heavy footsteps sounded behind me, and when I turned toward them, I found Rune, his large frame casting an intimidating shadow across the road. His narrowed eyes were locked on my father's face. "Bjarki Runarsson. I took my father's name when I left that life behind."

Surprise flickered through me, but it only lasted for a moment. His name change made sense. I'd always wondered how I'd never heard of him before. Bjarki, though, I'd heard his name so many times. A deserter, Erik had always called him. Someone who'd turned his back on the guild. But somehow, this revelation made me love Rune even more.

"Hello, Bjarki," my father said, folding his arms. "I must say, it's a surprise to see you after all these years."

"Hmm. Seeing as you came to the island knowing full well I was here, I'd hardly call it a surprise."

"You fled the guild."

"I did. Killing people for coin didn't suit me."

I stepped in front of Rune. "Leave him be. He's just trying to live his life out here, and he's done nothing to harm the guild."

"No?" My father's brow arched. "Then why is *my daughter* still here with him? Asking traders to make up stories about her death? Did he put you up to this, Frida? To get back at the guild?"

"No," I whispered fiercely. "I did it because I love him, Father."

His hand fell to his side, his eyes widening.

A rustling sounded beside my father, and I turned to find Logi walking toward me with a broad smile on his face. He flung his arms wide, then collided into me with a bear hug. A strangled noise popped from my throat as he lifted me from the ground, squeezing me in that rough brotherly way of his.

"I'm so happy we found you, Fri," he said. "And that you're happy and in love. I'm so sorry I ever asked you to join the guild. I knew it wasn't right for you all along."

The scent of brine swept over me from where it had clung to his skin and clothes during the long ship ride from the mainland. To come for me. To see me once more after thinking I was gone. Affection welled inside me, and I squeezed him back. I'd never dreamed that either of them cared this much. It had never even occurred to me that they might come looking. When I imagined the guild hunting me down, it had always been by the command of Erik. So that he could take me out.

But they'd come.

I looked over Logi's shoulder at my father. He

stared disapprovingly at Rune, his arms folded over his broad chest. As if sensing my shift in attention, Logi lowered me back to the ground.

I crossed to my father and took his hands in mine. "I'm sorry I told Louisa to lie to you, but you have to understand. I was trying to protect this place from the guild. Besides..." I took a deep breath to lend me strength. "I realized the guild isn't for me. I don't want to be an assassin. I don't have the heart for it and never have."

He searched my eyes, the muscles around his mouth tightening. "You could have come home and told me all this. There was no need to hide from me, Frida."

"You're not the one I was afraid of."

My father clenched his jaw, then swore. "Erik's a bastard. When we discovered he'd sent you off on his own personal vendetta, the guild had a vote. He's out."

"What?" My eyes widened. "You kicked him out of the guild?"

"That's right. And now I've taken over." He motioned at his mottled gray leathers—the leathers of the guild's leader. I'd noticed them before, but I hadn't acknowledged what it meant.

"Which means things are changing," Logi said. "No more vows. No more cutting people out."

My father nodded. "I made a mistake all those

years ago in not coming for you, Frida. I won't make that mistake again. You're my daughter, and I want to be a part of your life. It's what your mother would have wanted, too. So if that means you live here, and we visit from time to time, so be it. And you're always welcome back, if you ever want to visit us."

"You too, Rune," Logi said, grinning.

"Wait, do you truly mean that?" I looked from my father to my brother, hope blooming. "We can still see each other, even if I'm not joining the guild?"

"Of course, Fri. We just want you to be happy," said Logi.

My father gripped my shoulder. "Losing you once is my biggest regret. I won't lose you again."

29

FRIDA

The official start of summer brought the long days, the swarms of insects, and the sticky heat that could only belong to a tiny wedge of land fully surrounded by the sea. To battle it, every home spat out its inhabitants so they could lounge in the shade of the redwoods or the dozens of pavilions scattered along the street.

Rune and I strolled hand-in-hand through the throng. Occasionally, I paused to examine the wares of a travelling merchant, exclaiming at the beauty of their jewellery or their impressive embroidery. Many had dragon knickknacks for sale, thanks to the commencement of the first official Dragon Festival.

After meeting Eldi and hearing all about my island adventures, my family had decided to remain in Oakwater for a week before journeying back to the mainland, carrying with them the promise to send some of my things on the next ship out of the port: my Silva Sweetwater novels, my favorite dresses from my cottage, and my beloved horse. I couldn't wait to see Stella again.

Rune and I walked along, stopping at Lilia's Travelling Tavern. She'd set out tables and chairs beneath a canvas pavilion, decorated with looping vines and fresh flowers. Even though it was early yet, every seat was taken. I ventured up to the open window and braced my forearms against the wooden serving ledge.

"Hi, Lilia," I said. "Happy Dragon Festival."

She leaned toward me, her silver hair cascading over her shoulders. "Happy Dragon Festival, Frida. I'm so happy everything has worked out for you and your family."

Rune pressed a hand against my back. "I've just seen someone I want to speak with. I'll be right back."

As he vanished into the crowd, Lilia handed me a frothing tankard. "You know, I've known Rune for many years, and I've never seen him this cheerful."

I flushed. "Well, he makes me feel pretty cheerful, too."

She smiled. "I'm grateful for what you did for

Eldi. Reykur's been off visiting his sisters, but when he gets back, he'll be so thrilled his brother is flying again."

We both turned toward the dragon. He sat curled up in the middle of the festival, perched on a growing mound of gold coins. The beast was clearly basking in the attention. Folk kept wandering by and scattering gifts around him. He was even allowing them to touch his tail.

I smiled when Logi approached him and patted him on the nose. My brother had been beside himself when I'd first introduced them, and I'd half-expected him to remain here, just so he could see the dragon every day.

"He's certainly enjoying the attention," I said fondly.

"Finally," Lilia said. "After he got caught in a storm a couple of decades ago, he hid away in his cave and refused to see anyone. I thought he'd never come out, if I'm honest."

"So that's what happened," I said. "A storm?"

"Lightning even struck him. He was pretty badly hurt," she said sadly, then shook her head and brightened. "Nevermind about that, though. You got him out of that cave, and that's all that matters. Want one of these for Rune?"

She set down a second tankard. I took it, passed her some coin, and thanked her for the drinks. Then I wound through the crowd to find Rune.

He stood just beneath the drooping willow tree with his arms tucked behind his back, his cream tunic rolled up to his elbows and a dragon pin attached to his collar. The spark of light in his eyes made it hard to breathe. Looking at him made me feel like every wrong turn I'd taken was worth it, just to be standing in front of him now.

He was my home. The only home I ever needed.

"I have something for you," he said, his lips curving into a sweet smile around his tusks.

I walked toward him, something in my chest fluttering. When I reached him, he leaned down and brushed his lips across mine.

"Hmm. That's nice," I whispered, my mouth still pressed against his.

He pulled back. "Well, that's not your gift. This is."

Rune pulled his hands from around his back and thrust something toward me. It took me a moment to understand what it was. Something small and rectangular, wrapped in gauzy cloth. Shooting him a quizzical look, I took it from him, finding it surprisingly heavy in a very familiar way.

"Is this a book?" I exclaimed.

His smile widened. "Go on. Open it."

I tossed aside the cloth and drank in the words etched into the leather cover.

The Orc's Bride
by Silva Sweetwater
First Edition

I gasped.

Rune shifted on his feet. "Now I know your father is sending all your books here, but that's the one you said you didn't have. I hope it's the right one, anyway."

"It *is* the right one." I shook my head, staring down at the words. "There are only a hundred of these in existence, if that. They never printed a second edition because of the war. Rune, this is incredible."

He grunted. "I'm glad you like it."

"Like it?" I looked up at him, smiling with wild abandon. "Rune, I love this. It's the most generous thing anyone has ever gotten for me. It means the world to me to have this. How did you even find it?"

"I have my ways," he said with a secretive smile. "Looking forward to reading it?"

I giggled. "You have no idea."

He slid his hands around my waist, then tugged

me against his chest. "I just hope it doesn't disappoint you."

"How could it possibly do that?"

He leaned in, brushing his nose against mine. "Because no fictional romance could ever compare to what we have."

"Hmm." Sighing, I closed my eyes. "Maybe that just means I should put quill to parchment for our love story."

"And what would you call it? The Orc's Elven Lover?"

I smiled. "Built by Magic."

GLOSSARY

DRAUGR - those who bond with dragons and channel their power

FENRIR - wolf-like creatures who can form powerful bonds with folk

FILDUR - the elemental magic of fire

FOLK - beings in tune with the Galdur; includes elves, orcs, pixies, trolls, fenrir, demons, giants, kraken, and dwarves

FREYA - the ancient goddess of the elements

GALDUR - the elemental magic that runs through the bones of the earth; can be controlled by rare sand

GEMSTONES - gems that are mined by the dwarves, some of which have magical properties, such as sunstones

HUGUR - the elemental magic of mind/thoughts

JORDUR - the elemental magic of earth

MIDSUMMER GAMES - an annual celebration that takes place in Wyndale, complete with a tournament; the winner may ask for one gift from the island

THE OLD GODS - ancient beings who crafted the world and gifted the folk with Galdur

THOR - the God of Thunder, worshipped by the dwarves

VATNOR - the elemental magic of water

VINDUR - the elemental magic of air

YULE - the annual winter festival to celebrate harmony, bounty, and happiness, and to bless the coming year

ALSO BY JENNA WOLFHART

Falling for Fables

Forged by Magic

Brewed in Magic

Mined in Magic

Built by Magic

The Mist King

Of Mist and Shadow

Of Ash and Embers

Of Night and Chaos

Of Dust and Stars

The Fallen Fae

Court of Ruins

Kingdom in Exile

Keeper of Storms

Tower of Thorns

Realm of Ashes

Prince of Shadows (A Novella)

ABOUT THE AUTHOR

Jenna Wolfhart spends her days dreaming up stories about swoony fae kings and rugged blacksmiths. When she's not writing, she loves to deadlift, rewatch Game of Thrones, and drink far too much coffee.

Born and raised in America, Jenna now lives in England with her husband and her two dogs.

www.jennawolfhart.com
jenna@jennawolfhart.com
tiktok.com/@jennawolfhart

9 781915 537935